VAGABONE

By
Connor de Bruler

First Montag Press E-Book and Paperback Original Edition July 2021

Montag Press ISBN: 978-1-940233-93-2
Design © 2021 Amit Dey

Montag Press Team:

Editor: Charlie Franco
Cover: Deborah Zuanazzi
Model: Gabriele

A Montag Press Book
www.montagpress.com
Montag Press
777 Morton Street, Unit B
San Francisco CA 94129 USA

Montag Press, the burning book with the hatchet cover, the skewed word mark and the portrayal of the long-suffering fireman mascot are trademarks of Montag Press.

Printed & Digitally Originated in the United States of America
10 9 8 7 6 5 4 3 2 1

*"You got a one-way ticket to the promised land,
you got a hole in your belly and a gun in your hand."*

— Bruce Springsteen

The Teacher has fixed the morning's schedule. The compulsory lessons will be postponed--due to the impromptu execution of four men--and held later in the evening in place of the marksmanship class, which, having moved to the earlier slot, will serve as the means of execution. He instructs a pupil to take four books from the subversive repository and use a power drill to bore a small hole in each book's center and then duct tape them to the men's chests. Each is tied to a portion of the courtyard fence with a bag placed over his head. The children are issued their rifles and rest them on a row of sandbags at the opposite end of the courtyard. The aim is to shoot as accurately as possible in the center hole of the book. The Teacher sits behind the rifle instructor who gives the students to the count of three. When the class is over, the men slump to the side, still tied to the posts with blood-stained page fragments at their feet like torn leaves.

PART ONE:

The Great Western Thunderbird

1

Her morning starts with the gaseous burst of exhaust brakes followed by a shrill, intermittent alarm that echoes through the smoky lot beyond the motel door. The room is still dark. She can see the rear lights of the tractor-trailer as it backs into a loading dock through the foggy, bottom-floor window. The window's condensation reveals the finger drawings of the last child to stay there: a rudimentary horse, a house beside a silo, or possibly a chimney, a little girl's name, a frowny face. Through this vague, glass palimpsest, she can make out the woods beyond the lot. The world is void of greenery. She sees only brittle twigs and skeletal tree stumps wrapped in a mesh of leafless kudzu vines like twisted hair pulled from a bathroom drain.

She sits up in bed and then walks, barefoot, across the kind of floor that belongs in a theater lobby. She flips the bathroom switch with the back of her hand. Slowly, the mercury vapor tube above the mirror floods the space with light accentuating the cracks in the enamel sink and rust collecting on the edge of the faucet. She looks at herself in the meat-locker glow: undone hair, stained tank-top, gray panties. The sealant between the tiles on the floor is dry, frayed. Little tags of loose rubber scrape at her feet as she steps into the shower and again when she brushes her teeth.

She puts on some cleaner clothes and zips everything into one backpack. Her washed hair stands on its ends, thick and spiky with hard water and cheap shampoo. She puts on the inconspicuous green overcoat and pulls a red wool cap over her hair. She puts on the hiker's pack and clips the straps. The sun starts to rise. She heads outside with the magnetic room key in her hand. Another woman sits on the sidewalk as she smokes a cigarette, shivering in the dawn half-light. Amalin walks around her and doesn't make eye contact. She crosses the depot lot as a semi backs into another loading bay. The tarmac is already crawling with forklifts and men in reflective yellow vests, feds carrying machine guns, refugees, prostitutes, UN coordinators with laminated ID badges. She steps into the manager's office. The elderly Haitian sits behind the check-in desk pouring a cup of coffee from a large thermos. He had taken his holster off his belt and set the Glock beside the keyboard of the computer. She hands him the room key.

"You can open 112 back up."

He looks at the room key without touching it.

She stands in silence and grips her shoulder straps.

"I'll keep it booked until midnight tonight."

"You're a good man," she says, taking out a roll of glistening pink military vouchers. She peels off the amount for the next night.

"Don't bother," he says, "I'll roll it over when you come back."

"I'm not coming back."

He says nothing and sips his coffee.

She pockets the bright plastic slips and walks out the door. Outside, she follows the razor-wire fence to the outskirts of the depot until she can smell coffee and food. Burn barrels and a few open campfires fill the air with clouds of smoke and fluttering embers of weightless carbon. Lines are starting to form around each of the many tents as the huddled groups disperse. She ignores the Southern Baptist missionaries spooning out grits and scrambled eggs onto paper plates. In a few minutes, the preacher will plug in the sound system and, when it isn't blasting twenty-year-old Christian Rock, he'll start free-associating like a schizophrenic auctioneer. She passes a few more church-run tents. The Scientologists have French toast. Members of the Chinese government along with some Sri Lankan aid workers have eggs and broccoli, coffee and tea, a waffle station. She gets a cup of black coffee and takes a seat at the folding table under the UN spread. A man in a black and red checkered coat with a fur-lined cap steps over a child in a sleeping bag. He has a lanyard around his neck with his translator's ID. He approaches Amalin.

"English?"

"Yeah."

"You want a cigarette?"

"Where did you get'em?"

"Chinese diesel mechanic."

"What'd he give'em up for?"

"Pint of whiskey."

"Why'd you give that away?"

He sniffles.

"You want one or not?"

"I don't smoke. You got any more whiskey?"

He walks away without answering and offers his cigarettes to refugees in the coffee line. One by one, they pull from the pack. He gives most of them a light. Some place the cigs behind their ears for later.

A kid who doesn't look a day older than sixteen sits down beside her.

"You in the market for some hooch?"

"Fuck off," she says.

He stands up and disappears into the crowd.

She drinks her coffee and grabs some sausages once the line dies down. They have no flavor. She takes a few bottles of water from a communal cooler and stashes them in her pack.

Ashish, a UN worker from Tanzania (Nepali extraction), finds her as she sets her pack over her shoulder. He asked her once if she was part Indian.

"No," she said, "Of course not."

"No? Were your parents' hippies?"

She shook her head. Her parents were first-generation Mexican-American, devout Catholics.

"Your name is Sanskrit for purity, cleanliness," he said.

He knew this because of his name: Ashish, the blessing.

"Where are you headed today?" he asks.

She doesn't answer his question.

"That driver you had helped, the one from Lynchburg. He runs a Venture rig, doesn't he?"

Ashish nods. He says something but the noise of an engine's Jake brake cuts him off.

"What?"

"I said 'yeah.' The man with the knife wound in his stomach?"

"That's him. Do you know if he's back on the fleet?"

"I can't tell you that," he says. "What are you planning?"

She walks away.

She hitches a ride on the side of an empty forklift.

"You'll have to get off about 30 yards before the hot zone. I don't want to lose my job," the driver says.

"Just get me across the lot."

The wind assaults her cheeks as they weave around containers and crates, engines, fuel tanks, endless lines of electrical cord. She can feel the cold in her knuckles as she grips the safety bar. Once the aluminum tower is visible on the horizon the forklift operator stops dead.

"Alright, get off."

She climbs down and he jets away. His electric motor hums in the distance. She walks alone toward the gray monolith of the weigh station where the shipping containers are stacked more than three stories high. She heads left and approaches the squat building away from the trucking lanes. Behind yellow siding just above the unsullied glass, the black letters spell out, "Waffle House." There's a sign on the door that says, "No, MVs. Cash and Card Only."

She pushes the door open and enters the steam-filled room. Coffee bubbles in the glass pot beside the refrigeration unit.

Eggs and meat sizzle on the flat top grill. An elderly server turns to her.

"Just one?"

"Where do the Venture Logistics guys sit?"

She points to the far table.

Amalin walks over to the group of three men.

"Which one of you is from Lynchburg, Tennessee?"

An older man with a white handlebar mustache stares up from his coffee cup, both hands clasping the warm ceramic, elbows planted on the table.

"Who's askin'?"

"I'm carrying a message from Ashish. He just wants to find the guy with the punctured stomach."

The man on the right with a shaved scalp and hunting jacket jerks his head toward her in recognition.

"The UN nurse?"

"Yes," she says.

"Dark guy. Kind of short?"

"That's him."

The man with the thick mustache sets his coffee down.

"The one that sewed you up for free after that gaucho stuck you?"

He nods in agreement.

"That's him alright. What's his message?"

"He's just following up. He wants to make sure…"

All three of them start laughing.

The bald trucker stabs his hash browns with the fork.

"Is that so? He sent you?"

"Yeah."

"I got a message too," he says. "Tell him he should get his head looked at."

"What's wrong?"

He takes a bite of food before answering.

"Something's gotta be wrong with his head if he already forgot he checked the stitches yesterday evenin'."

She feels her cheeks burning.

The two others laugh.

"Did you not know that? Did he not say? To be honest, I wouldn't give a good goddamn if he walked in here himself and acted like I owed him. I don't give a fuck. I don't give a fuck about you or him or anybody else. And I ain't givin' no con artist the time of day."

"She's fishing for a ride," one of them says.

The server grabs her by the wrist.

"You can't be standin' in here if you ain't gonna eat."

She rips her hand free.

"I'm going," she says, "I'm gone."

3

Half the folks in the diner are yelling at her by the time she storms out.

She punches the dumpster out back with her bare fist and sits down on an upturned milk crate.

She sighs. Her breath is visible in the morning sunlight. The air smells like diesel fuel and kitchen grease. She hears loud footsteps behind her and half-expects the manager to kick her off the premises, though it's difficult to tell where the diner property starts and the station lot ends. She turns around ready to defend herself and sees a young man standing there. He keeps his distance. She vaguely recognizes him from inside the Waffle House and gets a better look; average height, thin, dark black skin, short hair. He wears a jean shirt with a bolo tie around the collar, jean pants, Western boots, a black-felt Stetson that shields his eyes from the sun, and fingerless wool gloves. He carries a Sig Sauer P226 in a leather holster at his hip.

"How much you got?"

She squints at him.

"Are you robbing me?"

He frowns.

"Listen, girl, I think fast and I act fast. I get the job done or I don't do it at all. You're lookin' for a ride. So, how much you got?"

"A grand."

"Let's see the money."

"Let's see the rig."

"My truck's getting a final inspection right now. After that, they're gonna load the cargo and place the seal. We're looking at two hours."

She stands up.

"How are you gonna get me into the cabin?"

"That'll be the easy part. I don't have the same eyes on me as the Venture Logistics drivers."

"Then who do you drive for?"

"I'm ARC."

"You're on contract."

"I'm the best there is."

"How old are you, fifteen?"

"Nineteen."

"You're kidding."

He places his hands on his belt.

"Alright, forget it. Con your way onto some other truck."

He turns his back to her and struts away.

She thinks for a moment and then follows him.

"You think you can get me past The Cordon?"

"Of course I can."

"You're willing to risk your income and three years in a prison camp?"

"Five," he says. "That's five years. They increased it last month."

"And you're not scared of that. What's in it for you?"

"Well, you're going to give me a thousand dollars, ain'tcha?"

She stops dead and takes off her pack. He watches her as she unzips the bottom and, briefly, flashes the roll of American currency.

"I have my own gun and knife that I'm not going to show you. If you try to steal from me or maroon me, or give me up to the authorities…"

He smiles and plays with the brim of his hat. There's reckless amusement in his eyes as he diverts his attention to the ground and kicks a piece of gravel across the tarmac.

"How are you planning to smuggle me inside?"

"Get a head start," he says. "Be in the flats in two hours. Meet me by the burned-out church, the one next to the old tree. You know which one I'm talking about?"

"I've seen it," she says.

"Nobody's out there on patrol in the daytime. I'll catch you there *if* you're there. If not, an MP spots you, you don't make it, I'm just gonna keep on ridin'."

"That's a bad plan."

"It's the only way I know."

"You've smuggled before?"

"I said I'm the best driver there is, didn't I?"

4

She hides inside a wide gulch, her back to a few diagonal lengths of splintered timber. Above her, the church's steeple is lopsided, curving toward the ash-covered ground in the shape of a claw. The front portion of the building is destroyed, the chapel and pews exposed. The steps that once led to the entrance are rubble. She keeps her head low and watches the faded road for the massive truck. There are no Jeeps, no Humvees, no tanks that she can see.

She sits alone and opens her pack. She hides the money and her roll of vouchers in a new place at the top of the pack inside a Velcro pocket below her bedroll. She pulls out the wood-handled Colt Python and her box of .357 magnum cartridges. The gun is always loaded. She stuffs it into the breast pocket of her coat with a handful of extra cartridges. Her stainless-steel knife is sheathed above her right ankle.

She takes out a yellowing copy of *Siddhartha* and reads through the first six dog-eared pages.

A diesel engine carries through the distance. Somewhere beyond the hill, death calls to her like a forgotten voice;

the promise of suffering. Black hills of desiccated, fossilized sediment go on for miles like the memory of an ocean scattered with the brittle imprints of what was once abundance. The truck peaks at the top of the hill and barrels down to the old church. She spots the black Stetson in the windshield and puts the book away, flagging him down.

The kid drives parallel to the gulch and stalls. She jumps up and climbs into the cabin.

"Welcome aboard," he says.

"Where do I hide?"

He points to the bed behind the driver's seat.

"Flip the mattress."

She stares at the small nook behind the front seats. It's just large enough for a raised bed and an overhead storage space hidden by a black curtain.

"What about the space up there?"

"No, don't go up there. That's the first spot they check."

She flips the thin bed below. It rests, suspended by four wooden boards, less than a foot above a shallow storage space. She says nothing and pushes the loose boards away, crawling into the tight space. She takes off her pack, wedging it beside her, and then shifts the boards back in place to support the mattress.

"Does it look right?" she calls out.

He pivots the chair, keeping one hand on the steering wheel, to smooth out the mattress.

"Looks okay to me," he says. "You like music?"

"Sure," she yells.

She decides to stop talking and lays her head back in the dark. The cabin is filled with classic rock from the aging sound system. There are brief flashes of light that reach below into the hidden compartment. She smells cigarette smoke.

The music is a perfect cover. If she sneezes or rustles loudly, no one would hear her. Five songs go by before she feels the truck begin to slow. She can't see anything but she imagines the razor wire fence and the military personnel pulling back the massive iron gate; the sickly men and small boys who hold machine guns and barely fill out their uniforms with lopsided helmets.

He kills the music.

She hears mumbling punctuated by laughter.

The engines revs.

The distant cranking of gears.

The cabin moves again and the music starts back up. She takes the gun out of her coat and holds it close.

Two songs later, the music shuts off.

"You can come out now. We're officially in no man's territory."

She lifts the corner of the mattress edge with the sight of the pistol. The cowboy kid still has the driver's window rolled down after talking to the highway patrol at the checkpoint. He has a pack of Gold Flake Kings on the dashboard. An Indian cigarette dangles from his lip. Both his hands are firm on the large steering wheel. His eyes are on the road. Amalin takes her chance, jumping out of the compartment. She presses the pistol against the back of his neck.

"I don't know where you were hauling this cargo to, but we're not going there anymore."

He laughs and keeps on smoking his cigarette, letting his arm hang out the side of the truck.

"Shit, lady. You don't get me, do you?"

"I have a gun to your throat," she says. "You don't want to test me; I kill for a living."

"Yeah, but you don't know how to drive a rig like this, or else you would have already shot me and taken the truck."

"I'm taking it now."

He shakes his head.

"No, you're not. You're giving driving directions is what you're doing, telling me where to go. I'm not an idiot and I'm not easily intimidated."

She takes the automatic pistol from his side and sits down in the passenger's seat.

"We're going where I say."

"Where is that?"

"The desert."

"I'm already headed that way," he says. "Unless you're commandeering my cargo, we can probably come to some sort of compromise."

"I don't care about your cargo."

"Then let's keep the same deal. A thousand bucks a ride."

"I can't do that."

He nods.

"That's too bad."

"You're lucky to be alive."

He laughs again.

"Stop tryin' to be tough. It isn't working."

She keeps the pistol on him.

"I like my gun," he says. "You don't have to give it back but can you put it away in the glove box there."

She sets her pistol down and takes his Sig Sauer. She ejects the clip onto the floor and pulls back the slide. The chamber is empty. She forces open the glove compartment.

He whistles.

"Winston, kill!"

A creature sprints out from behind the black curtain above the sleeping nook. A powerful jaw digs a row of teeth into her left forearm, cutting through the green coat. It takes another wide bite to better latch on and uses its muscular neck to writhe from side to side, tearing the flesh from the bone.

The kid reaches for her pistol before she can think. He hits the brake and kills the engine.

5

Amalin pays him the thousand dollars at gunpoint. The German Shepherd, the one he called Winston, stares at her from the cabin in silence, its eyes following her every movement. The cowboy kid lets her keep her pack and military vouchers, her bullets, her knife, but he keeps the Colt.

"I'm gonna toss this gun out maybe a mile and a half down the road. Good luck finding it."

He pockets the money and gets back inside the truck.

The engine bellows as she watches the rig disappear over the horizon.

She tears a shirt apart and sets her arm in a makeshift sling.

A pair of black vultures follow her, hobbling on every third step, coasting along the cold wind with their half-outstretched wings. The jagged fractals of their plumage glisten like shards of black crystal. The scavengers follow her for a mile down the road as she searches both sides of the faded, dust-covered remnants of the interstate for her pistol before abandoning her for the distant carcass of an unclaimed mammal. The pile of rotten carrion is encased in a layer of hardened clay as if sunken into a pond. There was rain when it died. She surveys the endless sweep of dead earth and rolling dust. This entire landscape is primed to become a deadly swamp in the event of a downpour and the sky is already a menacing, dark gray.

After an hour of walking, she finds her pistol beside the hollow trunk of what was once an elm. She picks it up and wipes off the grit. It's empty. She doesn't bother looking for the cartridges. If the kid didn't keep them, the wind has already scattered them. She sits under the stump and takes her time to reload and then breaks off as many branches as she can reach for a fire. She struggles to strap the roll of dead wood to the top of her pack beneath the bedroll. She snaps the plastic buckle and puts on the pack and keeps walking.

A few yards ahead, a beige house cat sits beneath a rock eating a small bird. It sees her and drags the bird away.

A tin shed surrounded by a waist-high barrier of woven brambles comes into view. She can make out a dying pit of hot coals over a tripod. There's nothing to hide behind. She takes a hard left, still parallel to the rapidly fading outline of the interstate, and draws her pistol. She treks into the inch-thick soot until the shed disappears and then continues until the light changes. She navigates back to the main highway and continues until dusk when everything between her feet and the sky grows a corpse-like adipocere of hazy blue twilight. There's a sprawling dead banyan ahead of her draped in its own twisted shadows like the silhouette of a biblical monster crawling across the sand. She steadies her right arm with her wounded forearm and the tension of the improvised sling as she aims through the sight of her pistol. She checks every gnarled root, circling the giant trunk.

She's alone. She finds a spot where she can rest her back and starts to build a fire with the twigs. She rips out the top portion of the copyright page from Siddhartha to start the kindling. She strikes a match and sets the stick into the paper. The fire spreads. The cone of twigs catch single flames and then collapse into a foundation heat, consolidating into one fire. She adds thicker branches and fire grows. Once the flames are high enough, she takes off the sling and rolls back her sleeve to check the bites. The punctures are scabbed over what little blood dripped along her arm is now fine crust. She feels her arm. It isn't broken. She moves her wrist and fingers. Her arm is bruised and swollen from the power of the dog's jaws.

She gets out the bedroll and settles beside the warmth of the fire.

*   *   *

She wakes up in the dead of night and draws the pistol on instinct. She's still alone. The fire hisses. She feels droplets on her face. Lightning flashes in the distance. It was the thunder that woke her. She gets up and, in the short bursts of light, sees a curtain of rain heading for her. The water appears to emulsify the ground. Her fire is rapidly dying. She takes up the bedroll and unzips the center of her pack where she keeps a blue tarp once used to cover a tent. She climbs up the banyan, fighting through the pain in her left arm, and sits on a thick branch. She wraps herself in the tarp as the rain falls harder. Soon, the fire is extinguished and the earth is covered with a foot of water as if the tree were in the center of a river.

In the first moments of the gray dawn, after the flood has receded, she crawls down from the banyan, the lone branch bobbing up and down from the absence of her minor weight, to the muck left behind. She abandons the sling and hooks on her pack and then tucks the edges of her pant legs into her boots. She trudges along. The sun barely emerges. The highway is impossible to see under the mud and soaked ash that cakes onto the worn tread of her soles. She takes out a stick of beef jerky and eats it and then drinks half a bottle of the water she had taken from the UN aid tent. She'd be lost soon. The road would bend and she'd lose it. She'd lost it before: once on a dirt bike in the same flatlands and once in the mountains, on foot, as she escaped a wildfire. Half the freight trucks navigated with old records of long-dead GPS signals never knowing exactly whether they were on the highway or not. Phony roads and new shortcuts crop up every day.

She was looking at sixteen years in prison for what she had done to the kid. She was lucky he was a loner. She was dumb and sloppy. Now, she had to pay for it.

She told him she killed for a living which was only half true. She said it to sound dangerous but ended up sounding weak.

It was her first contract and she ruined it.

A wooden log protrudes from the mucky ground. She sees it on the horizon and, slowly, recognizes the singular shrine for what it is. The log stands only slightly taller than a house. Its grooves and grain patterns are smoothed over from years of exposure like driftwood. A bent length of metal rests just under the rounded top covered a layer of rust: the nail that held a long-gone cross-section of wood to which the porcelain insulators were mounted. It's an old telephone pole. She studies it. A symbol has been carved into the side about four feet up. †: the mark of the Teacher.

*   *   *

The landscape reminds her of the coast, an endless beach at low tide. She sees a Bactrian camel up ahead. Pots and pans hang from a line wrapped across its humps. Its shaggy hide fans out like a mane across its long neck. Smoke rises from a campfire behind it. She keeps her distance, but the camel's rider, a gray-haired man in jeans and a green flannel coat, stands up and takes out a pump-action shotgun from the long holster at the crea-ture's side.

He yells "You tryin' to flank me?"

She raises her hands.

"No, I'm just giving you space."

"You tryin' to take my camel?"

"I don't want your camel."

"Alright."

He pauses for a moment but never lowers the shotgun.

"You got anything to trade?"

"No."

"Okay. You want some beans then?"

"No."

She walks until he vanishes behind her. She stays vigilant. He could follow her tracks in the muck for the next few miles.

7

The next day, she comes across a formation of giant rocks and smooth river boulders covered in dead patches of lichen where there had once been water. Fine brown sand near the dried bank kicks up in the wind. She crosses the long gulch of rocks and blackened tree roots. On the other side, a plateau emerges beyond the swells of fine debris. She climbs up a tall boulder the color of elephant hide. There're more trees ahead, more rocks, and steep trenches. The flatlands are gone.

She sits down at the top of the boulder and takes a drink of water. She screws the cap back on once she's finished.

A pebble smacks her knuckle.

Blood runs down her fingers.

Another knocks the water bottle from her hand. It rolls away to the edge of the rocks. A small boy with long brown hair runs out from behind a downed tree trunk and snatches the bottle.

She slides down after him as he takes off.

He wears a soiled white shirt big enough on his frame to be a tunic above thinning jeans. His department-store sneakers with Velcro straps are discolored from the sun and caked in sandy mud.

She fires a warning shot in the air.

He trips over an exposed root.

She checks her back as she closes in on the boy.

"Who else is here?"

The boy doesn't speak English.

"Don't kill me," he says in Spanish. "I'm just thirsty."

She asks the same question in Spanish.

"I'm only thirsty," he says.

She circles the boy, checking the tops of the surrounding boulders.

"I said, 'Who else is watching us?'"

"Nobody. I saw your water, so I took it. I'm sorry."

She kicks him over to look at his face. He scuffs his forehead in the fall. A narrow rivulet of blood runs down to the bridge of his nose.

She takes the slingshot from his pocket.

"This is what you hit me with?"

He nods.

"You're an accurate shot."

He says nothing.

She tosses it back to him.

"Get up."

"Don't kill me."

"I'm not going to kill you."

He stands to his feet. She picks up the bottle and hands it to him.

"Go on, drink."

She watches his gullet pulsate as he drains the remainder of her water. He gives her the empty bottle and she sets it inside her pack. She keeps the pistol at her side.

"What's your name?"

"Pancho."

"Francisco," she says.

"Just Pancho."

"Okay, Pancho. Where are your parents?"

"Under the ground."

"And you're alone?"

"I am now."

He looks nervous.

"How long?"

He shrugs.

"You're sure nobody else is watching us from the rocks here?"

He hesitates.

She points the barrel of the gun in his face.

"If you're lying, I'll kill you."

A rifle shot rebounds off the rock just inches above her head. The boy tries to run but she pulls him behind the closest boulder for cover.

"You liar. How many are there?"

"Please, don't shoot me. He makes me do this. I don't want to."

"Shut up."

She holds him close, pinning him to the rock, and yells out, "I've got the kid."

"He doesn't care if I die," the boy says. "And he doesn't speak Spanish."

She repeats herself.

Another bullet ricochets off the top of the boulder. She crouches lower.

"What's he want, Pancho?"

"Your things."

"Does he trust you?"

He nods

"I know I can't trust you," she says. "You're going to do something for me or I'll kill you."

He nods frantically.

"There's only one, right?"

He nods again.

She presses the barrel of the gun against his hand.

"I'll blow off your hand if you don't tell me the truth."

"There's only one," he whispers.

"Okay," she says, thinking. "The last few plans I had didn't work out."

She takes out the hot cylinder and shakes her remaining cartridges loose. She pockets them except for one and reloads it. She thumbs back the hammer.

"So you can't do anything stupid," she says. "He uses you like bait. I'm going to make you *my* bait."

"I don't understand."

"You take this gun and act like you shot me. Bring him down and get him close to me."

She fires the last round between the kid's feet and hands him the smoking Colt.

The boy steps out from the rock with his hands up, holding her pistol.

After a short interval of silence, she hears heavy footfalls approach.

"God damn it," she hears a man say in English. "She must've had you scared. I didn't think you had it in you."

"I killed her," the kid says in Spanish.

"Whatever the fuck you're saying, boy."

Amalin lies in the sand, playing dead. She looks at the older white man with a gray beard and a rattlesnake tattoo on his forearm through the strands of her hair.

He holds a lever-action Winchester.

"You did good, kid."

He pats the kid on the head and takes the pistol from his hand.

"Goddamn," he says again and spits.

He nudges her body with the tip of his jackboot. He turns to the boy and smiles.

She slices the back of his knees with her knife. As he drops to the side of the rock, she stabs him in the top of his right shoulder and again in his side. Struggling to pluck the blade from his ribs, she lets go and kicks the rifle from his grasp. As he rotates, she reaches for the handle of the knife, twists the blade, and pulls it free. Blood spills onto the sand. She presses his free hand against his chest and quickly slits his throat before shoving him into the dirt. He gargles as blood pools around his neck. She sheathes the knife and picks up the rifle and chambers a cartridge with the lever. He attempts to lift himself up. A thick stream of blood drains from his throat. She fires the rifle. His skull collapses, streaking across the next three feet of sand and rock.

The boy stares through the hollow crescent of the man's head.

She picks up her pistol.

"Who was he?" she says.

"Just a man."

"How long have you been with him?"

"A long time."

She pats down the corpse and checks the pockets. She finds car keys.

"What's this?"

"He has a Jeep," the boy says.

"Is there anyone else waiting at that Jeep?"

He sits in the dirt and looks up at her. He isn't afraid.

"No, you can take it. Can I have some more water?"

She reaches into her pack and gives him another bottle.

He takes a long swallow and gasps as he parts with the plastic edge.

"Come on," she says walking toward the shooter's perch.

"What?"

"Let's go. We're taking the Jeep."

He doesn't move.

"I'm not going to do anything to you. I'm not like him."

He stands up and follows her.

The Jeep is parked by a makeshift campsite. It has reserves of water, gasoline, and canned food stocked in the trunk and under the backseat. There are two more guns, both rifles but the supply of ammunition is dwindling. She empties the Winchester and counts the remaining shots. The boy takes a tin cup from the side console and pours himself another drink from the jug of water.

"He kept you like a slave, didn't he?"

The boy says nothing.

She reloads her pistol and checks the rest of the car. The man has half a handle of Wild Turkey Bourbon whiskey on the floor below the glove compartment.

"Are you from Mexico?" she says.

"I'm from Durango."

"That's in Mexico."

"Mexico?"

She hesitates.

"All the land south of...well...I guess it doesn't matter. How did you get up here?"

He points to the car.

"He took you from your parents?"

"He killed my parents."

She nods.

"Finish your water. We're leaving."

He drains the cup.

They drive until dark and set up camp at the bottom of a hillside. She heats beans in a brass pot over a fire and pours herself a cup of whiskey. The boy looks at ease. She sips the spirit and stokes the fire in front of them.

"We have too many supplies," she says. "We'll need to sleep in shifts."

"People take things," he says. "There were people even the man was afraid of."

She uses an old, wooden spoon to scoop the beans into a cup for the boy and gives him a piece of her jerky. She pulls the beans off the fire and eats directly from the pot with the spoon.

"Is that so? Who were these people he was afraid of?"

The boy shrugs.

"Come on," she says. "Who are they?"

The boy takes his finger and draws a swastika in the dirt.

She looks at it.

"You're sure about that?"

"Yes."

She draws the symbol of The Teacher in the dirt.

"You're sure this isn't what it looks like?"

He shakes his head.

"No, that's the Teacher," he says the name in English. "I know the Teacher. I used to live there with my mother and father before the man took me."

"You used to live there?"

"Yeah, we left to find food and he killed them and took everything."

He rolls up his sleeve and shows her the same mark branded into his shoulder.

"You used to live in the compound with the disciples?"

"I don't know what that means."

"There was a village with metal walls," she says. "A place where The Teacher gives his lessons."

"Yes, I lived there. I was there for a few weeks. We left Durango on a bus. Everyone spoke English. I don't remember much else."

"I've been looking for the Teacher," she says.

"They say everyone is looking."

"How would you like to go back?"

"Yes."

"Yes? You want me to take you back there. I can take you back."

He nods as he eats.

"Perfect. I'll take you back. I need to see the Teacher too."

He smiles.

"No one gets to see the Teacher."

"He might see me if I take you back."

He shrugs.

"Why do you need The Teacher?"

"Why does anyone?"

He nods.

"Then it's settled. I'll take you back."

She sips the whiskey and eats another spoonful of beans. The night sky is clear. She can see stars overhead. The fire dies down and her gaze returns to the swastika in the dirt.

"Do you know what that symbol means?" she says.

He rips off a piece of jerky.

"Yes," he says with his mouth full.

"They're still here?"

"Some of them. They're dangerous."

"I know."

She swigs the whiskey and thrusts the dregs of her cup into the fire. The liquor flashes.

Pancho finishes his beans and chews on the last scrap of leathery jerky.

"You were with the man for a long time, and you lived at the compound with The Teacher. Why haven't you learned English?"

"I don't know. We didn't live with the Teacher for long. I've been with the man longer."

"He didn't speak Spanish."

"No, he didn't. But I learned some things."

"Like what?"

"Bad things."

"What did he do to you?"

"He tied me to a tree with rope and waited for someone to help me."

"And then he'd shoot them?"

"Then he'd shoot them," the boy says.

"What else did he do?"

"I never got much water. I'm always thirsty."

She pours him a splash of Wild Turkey from the jug.

"Take this so you can sleep. I'll keep first watch."

The boy sleeps in the back seat of the Jeep while she monitors their perimeter with the scope of the man's bolt-action rifle. The boy wakes up screaming throughout the night. She wraps her coat around him like a blanket and pulls her red wool cap over his head. She lets him rest until dawn and falls asleep on her bedroll beside the charred pit of the fire.

When she wakes up, Pancho has rebuilt the fire. He has a green-enameled pot balanced on a pair of rocks amid the flames. The scent of smoke is too powerful for her to tell what the boy is heating, but the shape of the pot suggests coffee.

She sits up from her bedroll.

"I'm sorry," she says. "I didn't mean to fall asleep."

"I made sure no one was watching us," the boy says as he toils with the pot.

"What are you going to do if someone comes along? Use your slingshot?"

He points to the Winchester propped against the Jeep tire.

"That rifle will break your arm if you shoot it," she says.

"It won't break my arm. But it makes my shoulder hurt a lot."

"You've fired these guns before?"

He nods.

"You're lying," she says.

"I don't like lying," he says. "And I don't want to lie anymore."

She rubs her eyes and stands up to gather the bedroll.

Pancho takes a cup of cold water and pours it around the rim of the green pot to settle the grains and then pours her a cup of coffee.

"What is it?"

"Coffee."

"You know how to make coffee?"

"I had to make it every morning or he would hit me."

She smells it and takes a sip.

"That's good. Thank you."

He pours the remainder into a thermos and spills the dregs onto the fire. Steam and smoke rise.

She drinks her coffee and washes out the cup. Using the excess water, she brushes her teeth with her ration of toothpaste.

"You don't have a toothbrush, do you?" she says after spitting white foam onto the black coals.

He shakes his head.

She finishes brushing her teeth. She sterilizes the brush with whiskey and runs it under a splash of water from the jug and sets another strip of paste on the edge of the bristles before handing it to the boy.

"Brush your teeth."

He does as he is told.

They pack up the Jeep and settle into the front. She starts the engine and they drive across the plains of dying reeds.

10

Amalin stops the Jeep within a dry lake. The sky is a frigid, half-blue above near-black earth. A low moon hangs just above the tip of a distant snow-capped mountain. She gets out with the keys in hand and backtracks through the brittle crust underfoot.

"This is a bad place to stop," Pancho says.

"We're not setting up camp here," she says. "I just want to see something."

She kneels in the dirt and sees the massive tire impressions plowed by a freight truck.

"Do the headlights work?"

"One of them does," Pancho says. "It's a bad idea to use them. People see the light, they'll come for us."

She gets back into the front seat and starts the engine.

"They can hear us for miles anyway."

"It's still harder to find than a light," he says. "The man taught me that"

She turns on the single headlight and follows the impression of the truck to the edge of the lake. They cross a bald portion of a tall levee where the dry shrubs have been trampled and worn by traffic, a well-used shipping route.

"We're getting close," she says.

"Close to what?"

"The highway."

He stares at the mountain in the distance.

"I thought you were taking me back to the town with the Teacher."

"It'll be faster on the highway."

"The highway is dangerous. There are too many people."

She grips the steering wheel with both hands and feeds the engine more gas as they scale a hill of red clay. The road plateaus. She can see cracked slabs of asphalt embedded in the dirt ahead.

"I think we made it," she says.

"I think we should go around. Just keep heading south."

"We'll get there faster if we follow the road."

"The man always steered clear of roads."

"That's because he was a murderer. He didn't want to get caught. If we keep trying to find our way, we might run into more people like him."

Pancho goes silent.

She shuts off the headlight and drives for another few miles.

"We'll find a good spot to sleep for the night," she says. "I'll let you find it, okay?"

*　　　*　　　*

They park the Jeep on a tall slope overlooking the highway, hidden by tangled vines and dead trees. The boy's night terrors worsen. She listens to him with her back to the rear tire, the rifle in her arms. His agonized, hypnagogic wailing carries across the haunted valley. She imagines smothering him to death to keep him quiet not as a viable option, but a strange morbid thought passing through her unfettered consciousness. Afterward, she reflects on killing the man with the rattlesnake tattoo. Was she supposed to feel some way about it? Was indifference a natural response to gutting someone with a knife? It was a convenient response. She couldn't afford to carry any guilt. No one could, not in this world. Perhaps, she wasn't out of her element like she thought. She takes the knife from her ankle sheath and holds it under the moonlight. The glistening steel is still stained in dry splotches of blood. She chips at it with her fingernail.

11

She wakes him up just before dawn and bites a piece of jerky in two for their breakfast. He gnaws on the end while she stashes the rifle and starts the engine. They descend the slope toward the center of the barren valley where the highway cuts through the opposing tree-topped hills. Pancho watches the peaks in fear. The valley evaporates behind them as they drive through the plains. The highway remains intact for miles. She accelerates to seventy, the fastest she's driven in years, making good time. Pancho looks at ease once the high ground disappears. He keeps quiet.

"You have a lot of nightmares," she says over the roar of the engine.

He doesn't hear her completely and confuses the word *pesadilla* for *quesadilla*.

"My mother used to make me quesadillas," he says.

"No, I said nightmares."

"I don't know what that means."

"Bad dreams," she says.

He nods.

"I miss quesadillas. I miss cheese. Did you have a mom?"

"I did," she says.

"Did she cook?"

"She did."

"What did she cook?"

"Lots of chicken and rice. Rice and beans. Chorizo. But my dad liked Southern food. He liked to make pulled-pork barbecue with mustard sauce. Cornbread. Collard greens. He saw something in that stuff my mother didn't."

Pancho gives her a vacant stare.

"You don't know what any of that means, do you?"

He shakes his head.

"I try not to think about food," she says. "It makes me hungrier."

A red shipping container emerges on the horizon.

She slows the Jeep and pulls off the road, skidding along the plain. The upturned Venture rig comes into view. The crash looks fresh.

"What happened?"

"Looks like he lost control of his truck," she says.

"Someone set a trap."

"If they did, I don't see anyone around now. We just need to keep moving."

She returns to the asphalt and accelerates.

Pancho points to the mound of dirt up ahead. He says nothing.

"I see it," she says, acknowledging him.

The wind picks up, blowing the desiccated blades of grass across the asphalt like straw. The formation ahead of them isn't innate to the landscape. Its loose dirt piled high from some nearby trench.

She cuts a hard left, cruising once again through the plain.

He nudges her shoulder and points behind them.

She turns in her seat and sees a black pickup truck in pursuit.

"They're chasing us," he says.

"I know."

She presses down on the gas, leaving a cloud of debris in their wake.

The black pickup hangs back and drifts to the right.

"They're gone now," Pancho says.

"No, they're not."

She turns around and floors the gas pedal. The Jeep lifts into the air as they crest a hill. The aging suspension squeals. She nearly loses control of the steering and fights to center the vehicle.

The black pickup speeds into her periphery.

A pistol shot glances off the back just above the rear tire. Another one shatters her side mirror.

She steers to the left and speeds down a steep ledge to the low ground where she parks the Jeep lengthwise like a barricade before killing the engine.

"What are you doing?"

She doesn't answer. She pulls Pancho from the passenger seat and sets him behind the front tires. They can hear the truck engine bellowing as it reaches the top of the incline above them. She takes the three rifles from the backseat, resting the first over the rear door to peer through the scope.

The pickup roars along the top of the grassy ledge.

She fires a round directly through the driver's side of the tinted windshield.

The glass fractures.

She retracts the bolt, ejecting the cartridge and chambers its final round.

The truck rolls away as a side door bursts open and the dead driver falls to the ground, his legs still halfway inside as the truck veers down the incline.

She squints and aims through the scope.

A burst of semi-automatic fire from within the truck shatters what's left of the windshield.

Pancho covers his ears to muffle the screeching of pulverized metal as a hail of bullets rips the vehicle apart.

The smoke settles. Their gasoline and water reserves drain onto the floor and dribble into the dry dirt at their feet. Oil leaks from the engine. The chassis lowers as the tires deflate.

She drops to her stomach and crawls to the back of the Jeep, taking a shot at the new driver. The bullet sinks into his shoulder.

They duck under another torrent of machine-gun fire.

Pancho hands her the Winchester. She fires a barrage of deafening .30-30 rounds.

The truck careens toward them and crashes into the opposite slope beside the Jeep. She spends the final shots of the Winchester and picks up the last rifle, another cumbersome bolt-action. The doors open and another dead man slumps forward, dropping to the ground with his chin pressed to his chest in mid-summersault. A younger man, still child-like in his face, steps out from the truck with his hands raised in surrender. His head is shaved revealing a pink scalp untouched by the sun. A crudely etched tattoo of a German eagle stretches across his neck.

"Don't shoot!"

Amalin hesitates.

"Please, don't kill me."

He looks terrified.

She pulls the trigger but the rifle jams.

He sees his opportunity and reaches for the .45 in the dead man's holster.

She drops the rifle and jerks the Colt free from her breast pocket.

His hand wraps around the silver gun as two .357 rounds pass through his thin, hairless chest. His body falls back.

She stuffs the hot gun back in her coat, intending to take the .45 off the dead man, and turns to find Pancho still hiding behind the destroyed Jeep.

"Get up," she says, throwing her pack over her shoulder. "We have to run."

He climbs inside and searches for a jug of water without a bullet hole.

"Leave it."

She takes the silver pistol off the corpse, and the two of them race up the hill toward the tree line in the distance.

A second truck, a rusted, dirt-caked Toyota, follows them, passing the steep valley where the dead bodies lie among the smoldering, bullet-riddled vehicles. Its suspension conforms to the undulating terrain without jolting the gunner in the flatbed as they gain on them.

Pancho runs ahead as her adrenaline wanes and the sting of cortisol gives way to searing muscle pain.

The gunner in the truck bed fires two shells from a pump-action shotgun. The volley of buckshot misses her.

Amalin stops and calls out to Pancho. He looks back long enough for her to lob the Colt with four remaining shots his way. The gun lands at his feet. He grabs it and runs toward the thick woodland.

She falls to her knees and raises the .45. The gun is heavy in her hand, weighing down her extended arm. She pulls the trigger and the spent cartridge spins away from the ejection port in the glare of the muzzle flash. She smells the stench of cordite and scorched transmission fluid.

The gunner stands up from behind the cabin as he pumps a shell into the chamber.

She aims for his chest but shoots through his wrist.

His gnarled hand trembles as he leans over the top.

She aims for his skull and misses before moving her aim to the driver. He holds a revolver out the window and fires multiple shots, missing each time. His bullets kick up a mist of dusty earth, peppering her face. She returns fire and blasts apart the windshield. The driver ducks into the passenger seat amid the hail of glass. She fires another shot, puncturing the hood.

The slide stays back. Smoke lifts from the barrel and the open ejection port. She ejects the empty clip. The driver exits and moves in on her. She unsheathes the blade from her boot and lunges forward.

He draws a police-issue taser and hits her with the probes.

She remembers being hogtied. That much, she can remember: the steel cable bruising her skin, the corn cob gag hooked around her head by a wire coat hanger, being thrown into the truck bed with the gunner who wrapped his broken wrist in duct tape and kicked her in the ribs. She can't remember the edge of the camp, the Nazi camp. She wakes up in a cage, a makeshift holding cell in the middle of camp beside a cooking fire. She sees UN relief crates and drums of gasoline and diesel fuel piled together with no discernable order. A few wandering dogs sniff at the puddles of oil and scraps of chicken bones that litter the gravel. There's a loose pole in the distance just past the military tent flying the flag of the white ethnostate.

Her cage has thick rectangular bars, something animal control might have used to sequester a raccoon or coyote. She's still hogtied, but the corn cob has come loose. She spits it to the side and shimmies closer to the small doors of the cage.

A young girl walks out of the tent toward the fire. She holds a plate of food and a wooden fork. Her hair is unnatural, the color of an overexposed photograph. It's been cropped short with a knife, handful of hair by handful, almost like a punishment. She sits on a crate between the fire and the cage and shews the dogs away from her plate.

Amalin rolls over.

The girl stares at her.

"They talking about you in there," she says.

Amalin listens.

"They're calling you an Indian. You an Indian or something?"

She says nothing.

"They thinkin' you some kind of Cherokee or Choctaw fighter and they ain't tryin' to pick a fight with The Nation. But you killed a bunch of our guys, so they arguing about what to do with you. You killed my big brother. That's too bad. You didn't know that, so I guess it don't make it as bad."

She studies the girl's face and sees the boy she shot. They could have been twins.

"They don't want nothing bad to happen to your son. They say you got you a Little Tree still out there. He got away. You a mama?"

She nods.

"You ever read *The Education of Little Tree*?"

She nods again. She remembers the book. The author was a Klansman who pretended to be a Cherokee for the last leg of his life, getting his facts wrong, making up most of the indigenous words in his books. Mr. Agee played a radio story about it for the staff of The Bookshelf Inn.

"I get to read anything I want. We got lots of books here."

"I bet you do."

"I hope they don't kill you 'cause I never met no Indian before."

"Let them know, I'm not going to hurt anyone else if they let me go. I don't hold a grudge," she says.

"They'll decide what to do soon. They always know what to do. Would you like a bite of my taters?"

"Yes."

The girl reaches into the cage with the fork and gives her a mouthful.

The driver of the flatbed truck who shot her with the stun gun watches her from the opening of the tent.

"Greta! Don't feed her. She ain't starving."

The girl steps back and sits on the crate, turning her back to the cage.

Amalin lies on her side and stares into the fire. A light rain begins, dousing the flames. She thinks about her old life, her simple life. She dropped out of college at twenty-two and moved to Atlanta where she worked part-time at The Bookshelf Inn, Mr. Agee's rare volume bookstore when she wasn't bartending. The collapse was already close: mass graves piled up on the city's outskirts, the first suspension of the federal government, disease, the creation of the cordon. Mr. Agee shut down the store and moved to Florida to be closer to his children. He donated his books to a culture center in Tel Aviv to be locked away in a bunker. She thinks about the old lounge where she tended bar, the heat of the night rolling in from the open doors, jazz music, the smell of chartreuse and gin and fresh lacquer. She lived in a canary-yellow duplex on Meadowlark Avenue behind a chicken processing plant. They had a warped front porch with a corrugated tin roof and a banana tree that grew past the sidewalk. She used to burn incense to ward off the stench of chicken slurry and mask the smell of marijuana.

The flatbed driver taps her knife on the cage.

She looks up at him.

"What's your name?"

"Amalin," she says, choosing not to lie.

"Your son who's still out there?"

"Little Hawk," she says, lying.

"What about your husband?"

"What about my husband? He's dead."

She was never married.

"So Little Hawk ain't got nobody?"

"Nobody but me."

He walks away.

She waits for another few minutes. The little girl leaves her. She thinks about Meadowlark Avenue, the sound of the birds, the squirrels in the palmettos, the horn from the chicken plant marking a shift change, her pipe, her bag of weed, her bed, her black and white poster of the Arc de Triomphe, her collection of Mucha prints, her pile of books stacked high near the window still without a shelf, the succulents and cacti lining the sill, the Baphomet incense holder, the portrait of Henry Miller, the portable typewriter with single ribbon left, her laptop computer, her guitar, her DVDs, a soiled tinfoil tray of street-car empanadas, empty beer bottles, half a bottle of Mezcal, an old wicker chair salvaged from the roadside, the smell of another woman, the dildo in her bedside drawer, the branches in the windows, the Japanese lantern hanging from the ceiling.

Four men pick up the cage and carry her to the flatbed truck. The driver wipes the glass from the front seat and starts the sputtering engine.

Two men sit on the flatbed with her cage.

"Where are you taking me?"

They won't answer her.

They leave the camp behind and follow the road back to the crashed Venture rig. A few skinheads are already there, stripping the engine for parts. A taller man in a tattered jacket with a pitch-black swastika tattoo on his face approaches the truck as he lights a cigarette. He points to Amalin with the ember.

"She the Injun?"

The driver nods.

He rests his hand on the door as if he has the strength to keep the truck from driving away.

"Y'all turnin' her loose?"

"Yep."

"It were up to me, we just put a bullet in her now and throw her in the pit with Rick, Mark, and Davies."

"She ain't gonna do nothing. She ain't got nothin' left."

"Yeah, accept that little squaw hold up in the woods there."

"He ain't worth nothing."

"What'd you get off 'em?"

"Jerky. Box of .357. Bed mat. A tarp. Some clothes Inga can wear."

"She had plenty more than that if Mark hadn't used that machine gun. I seen what she had up there: gasoline, water, whiskey. We salvaged what cans of food we could and got the guns but..."

"Mark isn't alive to answer for himself anymore. It is what it is."

The skinhead takes a few steps back and spits. He stares at Amalin as they drive into the plains.

When they release her from the cage, they throw her from the flatbed and she lands flat on her face. The driver unties the steel cable like he's setting a wild animal loose, stands her on her feet, and gives her an anemic shove toward the woods. She looks back.

They aim their pistols in her direction.

"At least, give me my knife back," she says

"What knife?" the driver says.

She watches them, walking backward toward the woods.

Three pistol shots resound.

All three men drop to the ground in a red mist of blood.

13

She takes the truck keys and the two pistols off the Nazi marauders. Each one has a single bullet wound to the head.

"Where did you learn to shoot?"

Pancho shrugs.

"A little with the Teacher. But mostly with the man."

She takes back her knife and sets it in the sheath by her boot.

"You've got the best aim I've ever seen."

Pancho hands back her pistol.

"Toss it. I don't have the ammunition anymore."

He throws the gun in the dirt and climbs into the truck.

She wraps the seatbelt around him.

"So you don't fly out when I break," she says, noting the absence of the windshield.

"I waited for them, to see if I could kill a few more and steal some food. Then I saw they brought you."

She nods as she starts the engine.

"We got lucky."

She drives over the dead men's bodies. The cabin shakes.

"They'll come after us," Pancho says.

"Maybe, but I don't think they have any more power. They aren't organized like they used to be."

Pancho goes silent. He does that when he doesn't understand her. She can see it in his face. He's learned not to question anything; it's been beaten into him. He's a child of The Cordon, a prisoner of no man's land. It's all he knows. When life unfolds before him, the events pass through an empty vessel without anything to project back onto the world.

She stares into his eyes, his hungry, implacable eyes, and knows she can't help him.

14

Their faces are bathed in the dim green light of the dashboard gages. Amalin squints, staring above the tall steering wheel as the cold wind pours into the cabin. The undulating hills of dead grass give way to long, thin slopes of sand-colored earth peppered with strange, luminous deposits of ash that glisten white in their headlights like mounds of plucked goose feathers. It reminded her of snow. She tells Pancho to check the glove compartment for a Geiger counter. No luck. But he finds another gun: a snub-nosed revolver with a box of ammunition and a speed loader.

"We can't eat guns," she says.

The engine hums and the wheels grind as they scale a narrow ridge.

"I think I know where we are. The man used to come here when he killed someone and had money or things to trade. There's a place that has rooms and beds and sometimes food."

"Like a hotel?"

"He said that word a few times."

"Sounds dangerous. You think they'll trade a room and some food for one of these guns?"

"I don't know."

"Well, what did the man trade?"

"All kinds of things. Bullets mostly."

"Count the bullets in that box."

He opens the box.

"It's full."

"But how many?"

He slowly counts all fifty cartridges and sets them back in the dark box. He reads the red print on the front next to the image of a wolf.

"Woh-lifaeh," he says.

"Wolf," she says. "It means *lobo*."

She takes the box of cartridges and looks at the cartridge count and the words "made in Russia" along the edge.

"We can't barter these. It's too valuable to have a lot of bullets. We'll see what we can get for one of the other guns."

She reads the fuel gauge. They have half a tank left.

"How far is it from here?"

"Not too far."

"How do you know?"

He points to a strange formation of rocks on the left. It looks man-made like a shrine.

"I remember those rocks," he says. "You turn away from it and go down where the ground is low and then keep going until the trees come back."

She drives up to the rocks and turns, riding the break down the ridge. She follows tire-worn ground, the narrow path, alongside a tangled minefield of tree stumps and intertwined roots. The surreal landscape reminds her of a fresco she had once seen, years ago, in the Southwest on a pueblo church wall; something odd and supremely Mexican about its desolation, the entire world a desert. The moon and stars are absent from the sky. She imagines agave plants and tall growths of ocotillo rising from the loam, but this place is beyond death and possibly radioactive. Years ago, this might have been a vacant lot cordoned by a chain link or razor-wire fence with thick oaks draped in Spanish moss and wild sumac and tainted drainage-ditch reeds. Does New Orleans still exist, Miami? Her thoughts wander.

She drives until they have a quarter tank left. They stop on the outskirts of the massive antebellum structure. The majestic building stands alone in the bleached dust near eight tractor-trailers and a few sedans with modified tires. A floodlight shines from the triangular roof onto the makeshift car lot.

She looks at Pancho.

"Load the pistol and then give me the box of bullets."

Without hesitation, he loads the six-shooter, snaps the cylinder in place, and flicks the safety on muscle memory alone.

"Natural born killer," she says in English.

"What's that mean?"

"Don't worry about it. It's stupid."

He hands her the gun.

"No that's yours. Stuff in your pocket and pull your shirt over it."

She takes out the two pistols, both 1911s, and checks the clips. She stashes one in her coat and sets on the other in the cupholder between them.

Pancho shows her the speed loader.

"What about this?"

"Give that to me," she says.

They park the truck at the end of the hill and trek toward the building. Their footfalls crunch on the wet sand.

A short man in a motorcycle jacket sits on the steps with a carbine aimed at them.

"You a trucker?"

"No," Amalin says. "Just passing through?"

"Passing through? If you're not on a shipping route then what the fuck are you doing out here? We don't have time for trouble."

"I'm a woman with a little kid who needs some damn food and a place to sleep. I'm not trouble."

He used the sight of the carbine to point at their feet.

"Don't come any closer. You want a room and some food?"

"Yeah."

"You got money to pay for it?"

"I got an automatic pistol with a full clip I can trade."

He laughs.

"Are you shittin' me? That might get you a few drinks and a dry potato. You can't get a room for the night. "

"Just let us in."

"Give me the other gun you're hiding in your jacket and I'll think about it. That one loaded too?"

"That one's mine."

"That's not what I asked, you filthy beaner whore."

She takes out both pistols and hands them over. He stuffs one in the crotch of his pants and the other inside the open black pocket. He lowers the carbine and walks past them.

"Where are you going?"

"Back to my truck."

"Can we go in now?"

"I wouldn't recommend it. You don't have nothin' to barter with."

"I paid you."

"That's on you, you dumb bitch."

She looks at Pancho and gestures toward the man walking away with their pistols. He draws the snub-nose and fires. The short man drops to the ground in the light of the flood lamp as if he were on stage.

15

She pushes open the door to the dimly lit, smoke-filled room. The air stinks of stale beer and Chinese cigarettes. A rogue's gallery of haggard, sickly faces stare back through the darkness; truckers and wanderers, killers and con-artists who make their living beyond The Cordon. Pancho stays close by her side, his fingers grazing the pistol handle through his shirt. She approaches the rudimentary bar and nods to the elderly man pouring himself a shot of indistinct spirits.

"What do you want?" he says with an Eastern-European accent.

"A room for the night. And some food for the kid."

The old man stares at Pancho and sneers.

"Three-hundred dollars US. No Vouchers."

"How about this."

She places the 1911 on the bar top and stands the full clip beside it.

He picks up the empty gun and inspects it.

"I'll give you a jar of eggs and a piece of bread and one drink for this."

"No room?"

"No more rooms. We're full."

"Fine," she said.

"Just sit down somewhere, I'll bring it to you."

"We'll wait right here thanks."

He makes a muted noise clearing his throat and walks away.

She pats Pancho on the shoulder and leans against the bar top. The room has gone silent. The old man emerges from the back room with a jar of pickled eggs under his arm and a dish with a single piece of hardened French bread. He sets them on a small wooden table. Amalin and Pancho pull up the lawn chairs and sit. She breaks the bread in two and hands the bigger piece to Pancho and then reaches inside the jar and grabs a hard-boiled egg.

"Did you find your gun?" a voice above them says.

She recognizes the voice. From the shadows, she sees the outline of a black Stetson. A young man's hand reaches into the jar for an egg. He shakes the excess vinegar onto the table and takes a bite.

"I don't need any trouble," she says.

The cowboy kid pulls his chair up to the table. The German Shepherd languidly follows him and rests its haunches on the dirty floor.

"No, trouble," he says. "I got my money and you have your own thing going on. Just kind of interested to know how you got all this way so quick."

"Nazis," she says.

The room goes silent again.

"About six dead Nazis to be clear. But what do you care?"

"How's your arm?" he says.

"It's fine."

"Who's the boy?"

"Just a kid I'm helping out."

"You don't seem like the type to help someone."

"I'm taking him back to his people," she says.

"What's in it for you?"

"That's my business."

The cowboy kid makes eye contact with Pancho.

"You better watch out. This one's a backstabber."

Pancho keeps eating but doesn't break eye contact.

"He doesn't speak English."

"What's his name?"

"Pancho. What's yours?"

"Isaiah," he says. "Isaiah Dorman. And this is Winston, as in Winston Salem. You've already met him. I never got your name."

"You don't need my name."

"So what did you need to get past The Cordon for anyway?"

"You got paid. What's it matter?"

He finishes the egg.

"You said you were a killer when you tried to hijack my rig. You don't seem like a killer. You seem like whatever contract you're on, you're in over your head. So, what's the angle with the boy?"

She stands up and looks at Pancho.

"*Vámanos.*"

Isaiah flashes a key at her.

"I'll comp your lodging for one night," he says. "You sleep one night in a real bed, on my dime, and then you cut me in on whatever contract deal you have."

She hesitates.

"How do I know I can trust you?"

"Because I didn't kill you outright, and I made it easy to get your gun back."

She thinks and looks at Pancho.

Isaiah smiles.

"I'm the only one who's taking on a risk here."

"Why do you want in on a murder contract?"

"Money," he says.

"What percent?"

"Fifty."

"Thirty."

"I can do thirty."

"I'm not sleeping in the same room as you and your dog."

"I'm giving you the room. It's the last one. I haven't even seen it yet. I'll sleep in my truck."

She swipes the keys from his hand.

"We'll talk in the morning before we leave."

"I'll be here," he says.

She grabs the pickle jar and carries it to the stairwell.

The Eastern European man calls out to her.

"You want that drink or not?"

She turns back.

"Do you have clean water?"

"No, I have tequila, vodka, and some Greek licorice crap. Take it or leave it."

"Pour me a shot of the licorice," she says.

He reaches for the bottle of blue glass and sets down a cloudy glass for the shot. She watches him pour it and shoots it back.

*   *   *

They barricade themselves inside, pushing an old hardwood dresser against the door before sleeping. Amalin keeps a loaded gun on each nightstand in case someone tries to force their way into the room. They sleep side by side in the twin bed, facing the textured ceiling. The mattress is stiff and the rusted box springs creak like the inner workings of a failing clock.

Pancho finds a paperback spy-thriller in the drawer. He peels back its pages and a coin falls to his chest. He abandons the English-language book and plays with the coin.

"What is this?"

"It's money."

"Money? You can buy things with it?"

"No, not with that. Not anymore. It isn't much. It's the smallest unit of money there is. It's called a penny."

He plays with the coin, letting it catch the light from the crevice in the front door.

She tries to fall asleep first, knowing Pancho's night terrors would keep her up. The room is musty and the air is cool. She pulls the covers over her body. Pancho keeps himself occupied with the coin and she allows her consciousness to drift.

She wakes up not long after to Pancho writhing and kicking in bed. She touches his shoulder and he screams. Someone pounds on the wall in the adjacent room.

16

They head down the stairs in the early morning and drop off the key at the bar. The innkeeper, or whatever he was supposed to be, lies drunk on the floor and snoring like a dying peccary. Amalin steals the half bottle of real añejo tequila and takes back the 1911 with the clip. They walk out the front door and down the steps toward the car lot. Someone had moved the body of the man Pancho had shot last night. They follow the drag marks in the dirt to a smoldering pile of red-hot coals and with a blackened femur bone sticking out from the fluttering ash.

Pancho asks why they burned his body.

Amalin shrugs.

"Cleaner than letting it rot, I suppose."

She recognizes Isaiah's truck and pounds her fist on the door. The dog barks until he placates it and opens the door.

"Mornin'."

"Are we free to come inside?"

"That a house-warming gift?" he says, nodding toward the bottle of tequila.

"Sure."

Pancho and Amalin climb into the cabin.

"What about our truck?" Pancho says.

"We're leaving it. The Nazis might be looking for it."

Isaiah lights a cigarette and fires up the engine. Pancho sits beside Winston on the mattress behind them as Amalin counts the rounds in the 1911 clips.

"I've got a box of cartridges I stole from the white supremacists' truck. You think I can load it in these automatics?"

"What are those? Colt replicas?"

"These? These are Smith and Wesson 1911s."

"What's the box of bullets?"

".38 special."

He shakes his head as he takes a drag.

"I wouldn't. You'd need .38 Super at least."

"What kind do you have for yours?"

"Parabellum."

"Will these take that?"

"I don't know."

"We'll have to see."

He taps the filter of Gold Flake King on the edge of the window. The gray ash drifts into the ether.

"¿Puedo acariciar al perrito?"

Pancho asks if he can pet the dog.

Amalin turns to him and tells him not to touch the shepherd.

"What did he say?"

"He asked if he could pet your dog."

"He can pet Winston if he wants. If the dog thought he was a threat he wouldn't let him sit there."

"I don't want him petting him."

Isaiah laughs.

"So you ran into some Nazis on the road? The enthostate guys?"

She nods.

"They took me captive."

"You're lucky they didn't eat you and the boy. How did you escape?"

"They never got Pancho. Just me. They thought I was native and he was my son, so they let me go. Apparently, they're afraid of The Nation."

"Which one?"

"I never had to be specific. They believed me," she says.

"You killed six of them?"

"I did," she lies.

He flicks the cigarette out the window.

"Who's the mark?"

"The Teacher," she says.

He laughs.

"You're crazy."

"The boy is the angle. He used to live there before his parents were killed and he was taken by this pedophile marauder. He used him as bait to hijack supplies. I'm gonna return the boy to the village to get inside the walls and try to meet with him so I can put a bullet in his skull."

"Who's paying you?"

"Ex-senator who runs a collective in the North Carolina hills. He has clout with the military and a couple of Chinese shipping companies. He runs the east coast like King Rat himself."

"How much for the hit?"

"Fifty-thousand."

"If you ask me, he's playing you for a fool, selling you a dream. The Cordon is already starting to disintegrate, and when it does all hell is gonna break loose as everyone scrambles for the land. You think it's lawless now, just wait. He's laying the groundwork for his stake and he'll be damned if he lets anyone break down his capital."

"Then why are you helping me?"

Isaiah pauses.

"Not everything needs to be so easily understood."

17

In black hills where some living vegetation proliferates in small stalks of green sprouting through the crevices of a dry, soil-like crust, the diesel engine begins to sputter and buck. Once they're halfway up the near-intact section of highway bridge wrapped in an unfamiliar red vine, the truck dies.

Isaiah sets his hat on the dashboard and takes off his good shirt.

"I thought they checked your truck before you left the depot," Amalin says.

"They did," he says, reaching under his seat for a green-aluminum toolbox.

She waits alone in the cabin and takes a swig of tequila. She hands the bottle to Pancho.

"Take a sip. Just a little bit."

"What is it?"

"It'll help you sleep. We're gonna be here for a while. The truck is broken."

He sips the tequila and recoils.

"Lay down," she says. "Try to think of good things."

She takes another swig and screws on the cap. She doses off in her seat until Isaiah returns from the engine, throwing the toolbox back into the cabin, jolting her awake.

"What happened?"

"Fuel injectors are worn out. I need at least two or three new ones to get us going again."

"What about your cargo?"

"What cargo? I already dropped it off."

"That was fast."

"I told you I'm the best. Maybe that's why the injectors are so fucked."

"Who would trade a part like that with you?"

He gives her a look.

"Those things are worth their weight in gold. They're like tires or fuel."

She rubs her nose.

"So, we have to rob somebody."

"Head back to the pit stop and steal them from someone's truck."

She sighs.

"Is it better to go in the day or the dead of night?"

"I'd imagine the night," he says.

"We've been driving since morning. You're gonna walk all that way?"

"Hell no."

*   *   *

He opens the doors to the storage container and climbs into the darkness. She waits at the threshold and he returns with a dirt bike.

"Emergency vehicle," he says. "It's in my contracts."

"Nice."

"Help me get it down."

He rolls the front tire forward, gripping the seat. She takes hold of the handlebar throttle and eases it onto the road. Isaiah jumps down from the truck and closes the doors.

She hands him the toolbox.

"If I'm not back by tomorrow morning, keep walking," he says.

18

She doesn't let Winston sleep on the mattress beside Pancho. Instead, the dog sleeps on the floor between them. Amalin reclines in the passenger seat and dozes off for almost an hour before Pancho's night terrors commence. The shepherd barks at him as he screams himself awake and then growls and whimpers. He falls asleep again and just when the dog begins to calm down a light shines through the windshield. She looks out and sees the red-hot streak from a flare gun reach toward the starless sky and diminish.

She waits a moment, staring into the dark.

Another shoots upward.

She takes out a pistol and racks the slide and rests it on the dashboard before dozing off again. She wakes up in the middle of the night. It's raining hard. Thunder crashes over the truck and streaks of lightning glance off the edges of the abandoned highway bridge. They're on high ground, she figures. The water might rise up beneath them on the mainland, but not all the way to the bridge.

She hears Winston growl. She looks back at Pancho and sees his face in the next flash of lightning. He sleeps soundly amid the loud rain and continuous thunder. He looks peaceful. Isaiah's dog isn't growling at him. The dog stares straight ahead through the windshield, growling at the rain, at the darkness, and the intermittent glimpses of asphalt and wind-blown debris. The thunder crashes.

She doesn't know how to placate the dog. Amalin hadn't grown up with dogs before the big fallout. Her parents were not acclimated to dogs and didn't want to change when she was growing up. By the time she left home, a dog seemed too expensive. It seemed cruel to keep a dog cooped up in the house all day when she knew she wouldn't have the time or energy to walk it or take it outside.

She can't tell if it senses something or simply doesn't like the storm. The lightning flashes. The dog whimpers.

"What do you want?"

Does it need to piss? To eat? She doesn't know what Isaiah feeds it or where its food might be hidden in the cabin.

"I don't know what you want."

It yelps and then growls. Pancho rustles in the bed. Amalin opens the glove box and finds a tactical flashlight. She shines the light through the windshield. The rain falls straight. Two small rivers of dirty rainwater drain downward on each side of the highway bridge.

19

She wakes up at first light. The truck is surrounded by thick fog. Pancho and Winston are both asleep. The dog dreams, trotting its feet in the air as it lies on its side. She takes the pistol and opens the door and steps down from the cabin onto the slick asphalt. The air is damp and cold and smells like copper. She walks behind the empty trailer and lowers her pants to urinate, squatting low beside the tire. She pulls her pants up and buckles her belt as she looks over the concrete barrier at the foggy vista of crags and mucky terrain. She imagines smoke from the gulch where she saw flares but it's lost to the greater mist. The silence is interrupted by the stiff clip-clop of hooves at the far edge of the bridge. An old man riding a mule emerges from the fog. He's wrapped in a ghillie suit and wears a camouflage-print floppy hat. His belongings are stuffed in a gym bag pinned to the saddle horn. He stops.

Winston's muted barks fill the silence between them.

She holds the pistol, her finger flat on the trigger guard.

The old man's hands are empty except for the reins.

"Mornin'."

She says nothing.
"You broken down?"
She shakes her head.
"Alright then."
She watches the mule vanish into the fog.

20

Isaiah returns on the dirt bike in the afternoon with a can of stolen fuel and a row of salvaged injectors wrapped in a black plastic bag.

"You're still here?"

"I thought I'd give you another day just in case," she says.

It takes him until nightfall to get the truck to start. He sits in the front seat and starts the engine with his grease-caked hands, exuberantly clapping them together over the deafening hum.

He lets Winston defecate in the road and wipes his hands clean in a puddle of rainwater before they continue in the night.

Isaiah passes a canteen to Pancho and then to Amalin.

"It's sweet," she says.

"Electrolytes."

She nods, takes another pull, and hands it back.

"What did you do through the storm?"

"I found a dugout and stashed the bike."

"Were there any Nazis at the inn?"

"No, just the usual crowd."

"Backaways, they took out a Venture rig and cannibalized it for parts," she says.

"Probably cannibalized the driver too."

She rolls her eyes.

"Yeah right. They're not eating anybody out there."

"You don't think that happens?"

"Sure it happens. If you're desperate. But they're not eating people all the time. The little girl I saw out there had potatoes on her plate."

"Potatoes? Where the hell are they growing potatoes?"

"Looked like they had hijacked some UN relief aerial drops."

Amalin leans back in her seat.

Pancho sits upright on the bed beside Winston, scratching him behind the ears.

"They ate Winston's mother and father," Isaiah says.

"Neo-Nazis?"

"No, they weren't from the ethnostate. It was a group of pipeline guys stranded in the plains. They burned through their rations like idiots and got desperate, ate their guard dogs. I was stealing fuel and Winston tagged along with me ever since."

"What did you do before everything started to collapse?"

Isaiah laughs.

"What do you mean 'what did I do before?' I'm nineteen. Hasn't been a normal day in my life."

"I forgot how young you are."

"The world before? It sounds boring. Sit around all day. Sit behind a desk if you're lucky. Go to school. Listen to your president."

"You could have still been a trucker," she says.

"And for what? I'd rather be out here."

"You have a death wish, don't you?"

"Maybe I'm just not afraid of things that I can't control. Live fast, think fast."

"Maybe that switch in your brain just doesn't fire correctly," she says.

The cabin shakes from a dip in the road.

"You can't be nostalgic for something you never had," Isaiah says, hands tight on the wheel.

"Sure you can. As long as you know it existed at one point, you can want it."

Isaiah taps the pack of Gold Flake and pulls one out with his teeth. He lights it and rolls down the window, blowing the smoke.

"What about you? What did you do 'before?'"

"I was a waitress at a restaurant, then I worked at a bookstore and I tended bar at night."

"Like back at the Inn?"

"Yeah, but not shitty," she says. "I wanted to be a writer."

"A writer? And now you're a hired killer."

"Yup," she says, closing her eyes.

21

The village, or compound, whatever The Teacher's group chose to call it, is itself cordoned off from the main highway first by a series of dormant bulldozers wedged at strategic intersections of rock and cliff, which control the path of approaching vehicles, and later by a ten-foot-high fence of razor wire with a single checkpoint. Beyond the checkpoint, there is one path--a single lane strip of poorly laid tarmac--to the immense metal walls that circle the plaza and courtyard. Everything else outside of the lane is taken up by a maze of concrete barricades.

The young man at the checkpoint wears quasi-military fatigues and tan dungarees heavy with stuffed pockets. He wears a hand-sewn badge on his left breast pocket: a red cross on a white background. He carries an AR-15.

Isaiah rolls down the window.

"What do you got in the truck?"

"A dirt bike. Some pallets."

"The fuck you doing here?"

Amalin cuts in.

"We're returning the boy. He came here years ago. His parents were killed on an excursion for food and he was kidnapped."

"You're returning a boy?"

"He said he used to live here."

The young man walks back to the small shack at the gate. He speaks into a radio mic.

They wait.

He takes his time walking back and points to Isaiah.

"You, step out and open up the trailer."

Isaiah jumps down.

"Slow!"

Isaiah raises his hands and slowly heads toward the back.

Amalin scratches her chin. She waits as Isaiah opens the bare trailer for the young guard.

The two of them return. Isaiah climbs back into the truck.

The guard points to Pancho.

"Let me see your arm."

Amalin rolls up Pancho's sleeve and shows him the brand.

The guard scrutinizes the healed-over brand.

"Wait here."

He heads back to the shack and talks into the radio mic again.

Pancho looks at Amalin.

"I don't want to go anymore," he says. "I want to stay with you."

"You can't. It's not safe."

"I saved you. I'm a better shot than you."

"I can't take you with me. You belong here."

"I don't remember it here. I don't know anyone. I don't speak the language."

"You'll learn," she says.

"Who I'm I going to stay with here?"

"I don't know."

"Let's just leave," Pancho says.

"We can't. I need to see the Teacher."

The guard steps back to the side of the truck and makes eye contact with Amalin. He hesitates before speaking.

"The boy's welcome to repatriate," he says. "Have him step down and we'll have someone escort him inside."

"We'll do no such thing. We want to make sure he's okay. We'll escort him inside."

He gives her a dead-eyed stare.

"No."

"No? Look, he's agitated. I can't just abandon him at the edge of the wall. I want to make sure he's okay before I leave him somewhere."

"Then why bring him here in the first place?"

"He asked us to. He's just a kid. You have to understand."

He shakes his head.

"This isn't a daycare center. Outsiders don't get in. Period."

Isaiah looks at Amalin and then the guard.

The guard reaches out his hand.

"You can give me the kid, or you can leave. Those are your only options."

She hesitates.

The guard drops his open hand and raises the AR-15.

"Then clear out, back it up."

A pistol shot explodes from within the cabin. The guard's head bursts, splattering fresh blood and skull matter across the door of the truck. His body falls forward. A dark red pool steadily accrues.

Pancho shoves the smoking pistol back into his pants.

22

A small squadron of guards surrounds them as Amalin gives up her guns and raises her hands in surrender. She falls to her knees on the warm, sun-bleached tarmac strip. Jumping down from the cabin of the truck, Isaiah walks ahead of her with Winston barking by his side. He refrains from drawing the gun on his hip. They take the boy first and shoot Winston. The dog whimpers. Its body twitches and then falls on its side next to the expanding pool of blood from the dead checkpoint guard.

"This is a mistake," she says. "The boy doesn't speak English. He thought he was going to shoot us. He's disturbed. It was self-defense."

Another guard, his face obscured by a bandana, breaks her nose with the stock of his Bushmaster. Two others beat Isaiah to the ground. Amalin takes a steel-toed kick to the ribs and falls flat. Her hands are tied behind her back with sharp wire. They pull a pillowcase over her head as she's forced back to her feet.

She's led forward, toward the fortified compound.

"Listen to her. We didn't want anyone to get shot. We were trying to help!"

They punch Isaiah somewhere. The groin or the gut, either way, he stops speaking.

She is forced down a series of hard, damp steps. The temperature drops in the air but her cheeks and forehead are hot. Her blood surges. Her nose throbs. Her teeth feel chilled and loose. She takes each step forward as she's guided by two men. The noise of a dozen boots on the slick ground echoes as if they've entered some kind of narrow cave. She smells the musk of body odor, sweat, and smoldering carbon. Light pierces through the white of the pillow case. She's thrust forward. Her head crashes against a solid, cold wall; stone or crumbling brick.

She lies there for hours, listening to distant footsteps and water dripping from the ceiling. The noise of water isn't so much a monotonous torture as it is a revelation. Does the Teacher have access to abundant water? Had they installed a pump system? Does it come from a well? Are the drips only from the inherent moisture in the ground? She listens to every drop. Can it be cleaned? Does it carry disease? Does it taste like clay and sulfur?

The day slips away. She sits up. The wire constricts her blood flow. Her hands are numb from the wrist down.

The sound of a rusted hinge breaks the silence. Heavy footfalls descend upon her. She's pulled to her feet again. They push her forward; more walking, meaningless walking. They pull off the pillowcase and clip the wire around her wrists. The blood rushes back into her hands and fingertips. They toss her into a stone cubicle and lock the solid metal door behind her.

23

A small pressure lamp lights the cell. The silhouette of another person sits up in one of the two musty, moth-eaten cots. They pull the lamp closer to illuminate the hard wall where they scrape at the stone with the sharpened edge of a toothbrush.

"You digging your way out?" Amalin says.

The stranger laughs.

"I don't know what kind of rock this is, but it's dense. No, I'm just decorating."

She shines the light on the wall and shows Amalin the half-finished design.

"A totem?"

"It's gonna be the Thunderbird."

She sees it now.

"Impressive."

"You don't have to be a bitch about it."

"Fuck you."

The stranger laughs.

"I think you and me are gonna get along just fine. Let me give you the tour."

She sets the lamp between them on a stump of petrified wood beside her cot. She has a kitchen lighter and a bottle of kerosene and a single book. She extends her hands.

"This is it."

Amalin takes a seat on the opposite cot.

"I'm surprised they let you have a Coleman lantern in here?"

"The ceiling is high and there's an opening at the top, so we're not going to die."

"We could tear up the sheets and make a grappling hook to get out."

"You go ahead and spearhead the project," she says "I don't remember you from above. What did you do to get down here?"

"I'm not from above. I got thrown in here just today."

"The fuck did you do?"

"Somebody I was with shot a guard. It was a misunderstanding."

"All of the world's problems come from misunderstandings. I go by Madison. What's your name?"

"Amalin."

"Ooh, I like that. That's good shit."

She studies Madison's face as she smiles. She's missing a bicuspid and her front teeth are chipped and separated by a congenital gap which gives her mouth an empty look. Her hair is long and braided on one side. She has feminine features but her face is covered in a five o'clock shadow.

"You're sizing up my gender, aren't you?"

"Yes."

"Suffice it to say, that's why I'm down here."

"The Teacher's against it?"

"What do you think?"

Amalin stretches her arms.

"How long you been down here?"

"I don't know. A few months."

"They let you out ever?"

"Sometimes. That's when I get to shower and shave. I've been raped a few times, so get ready for that."

"I'm not gonna let that happen."

"When it happens it happens. You won't have a choice no matter how much you fight back."

Amalin pulls the knife from the sheath in her boot.

"We'll see about that."

"Holy shit! How'd you get that past them?"

"I didn't even try. They were sloppy. The next one of them I see is getting this right in his jugular."

"Keep it in your pants, Tiger."

Amalin sheaths the blade.

"What is this place?"

"I think it was an old textile mill, the basement at least. Now it's the 'detention center'."

"Smells wet. They have running water?"

Madison nods.

"The Teacher is obsessed with rudimentary amenities and medieval technology, ancient Egypt. Shit like that. They've been working hard on some running water, plumbing, what have you…"

"It doesn't smell clean."

"It isn't. They've been looking into a filtration system."

Madison notices Amalin's nose.

"They bopped you good."

"It's probably broken. It hurts like a bitch."

"We should set that before the swelling gets worse."

"You a nurse?"

"Nope."

"Have you set a nose before?"

She nods.

"How often do they feed you here?" Amalin says.

"Tomorrow morning a scrap of goat or chicken meat with old potatoes will slide through that slat."

"What about water?"

"Hold your mouth open during your weekly shower as much as you can."

"Shit."

"Seriously, you should lie down and let me set your nose while it's still broke."

"No anesthetic?"

"You can huff some of my kerosene."

"Can't we use that to blow a hole through the door?"

"Kerosene doesn't burn like that. It's not gasoline. Now lay down."

Amalin lies face up on the cot. Madison takes the blunt end of the toothbrush handle and inserts it into her nose.

"What are you doing?"

"Making sure I can find the airway."

She takes out the plastic and inserts it into the opposite nostril.

"It's lucky I had such a small toothbrush. If they gave me one of the thick grips with the rubber on it, we'd be up a creek."

She forces the end deeper into her nostril, prying the bone forward. Amalin grips the metal frame of the cot and grits her teeth.

"That hurt?"

"What do you think?"

She aligns the cartilage with the bone and pinches the upper bridge of her nose together.

"I think I've got it."

She lets go.

"You think you got it?"

"It looks straight to me. It's gonna swell up more and it's gonna hurt even worse. After that, it'll itch. Don't mess with it."

24

Amalin wakes up in the middle of a nightmare to feel Madison pulling the knife out of the sheath within her boot. She grabs her throat and slams her against the wall.

Madison struggles to speak as Amalin chokes her. She lets her go, pushing her to the ground.

"I just wanted to finish my bird. You know, on the wall?"

"These walls are going to ruin the blade. I need it to get out of here."

"You won't get out of here. They'll shoot you before you can get close enough to kill anyone with that."

Amalin runs her fingernail across the blade.

"I've gotten out of worse places."

"Yeah? Like where?"

"I was kidnapped by men from the old White Ethnocratic Nation, what's left of it. I got out of that. I can get out of this."

"Neo-Nazis," she says, wiping her face. "These are the real Nazis. This place is worse than you can imagine. They're gonna run the whole continent someday. People like you and me aren't welcome to be a part of that. We're gonna die alone, alone here with each other."

Amalin sighs and sits down on the edge of the cot. She takes Madison's toothbrush handle and shaves back a few light flakes of plastic, whittling a fresh point.

Madison remains on the ground, afraid to move.

Amalin blows away the last curled length of white polymer and tosses it to her.

"Here," she says. "Try that out."

Madison catches it.

"Thanks."

Amalin reclines on the cot.

"I wanna see the Thunderbird when you're finished."

25

A few bands of raw sunlight pierce the high stone ceiling. Amalin opens her eyes and stares at the elaborate, somewhat Aztec bird scratched into the wall beside Madison's sleeping frame. Its body is divided into compartments, each containing another symbol or natural scene. The wings are especially detailed: the feathers built from Latin, Runic, and Indigenous lexigrams. The bird's face has a nautical quality--vaguely hieroglyphic in its simplicity compared to the rest of the etching--like the art of the Wakashan-speaking peoples. She must have worked on it all night. She still holds the toothbrush handle in her blistered hand, having worked it down to half its original length. Her rags are covered in chalky dust.

She imagines that Madison might have been an artist in her former life. She thinks they might have been good friends if she had known her in the olden days, the abundant days. She lays her head back and focuses on the spiraling dust and fantasizes about climbing the high walls to the ceiling where she could crawl free. But the walls are smooth with nothing to hold onto. She turns again to Madison's bird. At least she has something to look at.

Madison wakes up and stretches her arms.

"That's a nice bird."

"Fuck you."

"No, I mean it. I don't know what you'd call it. An engraving?"

"Prison art. Post-culture art."

"Were you an artist?" Amalin says.

"I was something. What were you?"

"It's not what I was. It's what I am now."

"Ooh, so ominous. The fuck you talking about?"

"I came here because I'm a hired killer."

"Yeah?"

"I was paid to kill the Teacher."

Madison glances at the four walls of the cell.

"Great job."

"I need you to help me."

Madison rolls her eyes.

"I need to get a hold of the guards' guns. What can we do to get them to open the door?"

She shakes her head.

"There's nothing. If they suspect an ambush, they'll gas the whole cell."

Amalin gestures toward her knife.

"Your knife isn't going to save you. Maybe if you had a grenade."

"What about the lantern?"

"I've told you. It won't explode. It just bursts into flames. The only people it'll kill is us."

Amalin reclines on the cot.

"When do they give us showers?"

"Should be one coming up in a couple of days."

She nods and thinks for a moment.

"What is the Thunderbird?" she says, pointing to the etching in the wall.

Madison smiles as she looks up. Her eyes follow the dust motes.

"It's some Kiowa legend, I think. Or Mojave, I can't remember which. It's supposed to be some giant bird that used to pick men off the ground."

"The California condor?"

"Bigger. I don't know. Other people said it was a pterodactyl."

"Did you draw back in the day?"

"Back in the day. Like it was that long ago."

"Hey," Amalin says. "The guy I was with was only nineteen. His whole existence was like this. The kid I brought back must have been six or seven."

"You came with other people?"

"Yeah, a long-haul trucker I bribed to get me past The Cordon and a kid I found in the desert to use a bargaining chip."

"Bargaining chip?"

"Pretend like I was handing him over to the village. Maybe, he'd help me get close to the Teacher."

Madison shook her head.

"Your plan didn't work."

"Thanks. I hadn't noticed."

"Well, you're talking about yourself like you're some kind of badass, but you're just sitting here, you're just sitting here with me."

The slide in the base of the door opened and a small plate with two burnt potatoes and a stick of indistinguishable dried meat between them passed through. The slide shut.

Madison got up and handed Amalin her half of the food.

"This trucker you came with, the nineteen-year-old, you uh...with him?"

"No, matter fact he might try to kill me once the money's paid."

"He brought an eighteen-wheeler to the outskirts?"

Amalin nods as she takes a bite of potato.

"They've probably cut it up by now."

"Not likely. They'll use it though. They'll find some use for it. But he won't get it back."

"He's black," Amalin says. "Will they kill him for it?"

"I don't know. If they do, the Teacher won't say that's why, you know? He'll make up another reason for it."

She chews on the meat.

"How's your nose?"

"I'm talking a lot so I don't have to think about it."

"It hurts?"

"Yes, it hurts."

"It's crazy swollen."

"It feels like I have a tumor on my face."

"It'll go down eventually."

26

"**P**sst."

"What?" Amalin says, leaning toward the lamp light.

"Something occurred to me."

"What?"

"What if you're a plant. You know, an actor. What if they put you in my cell to get information out of me? And when you do, you'll kill me with that knife."

"Not likely."

"Likely? You kind of sound like the rest of them."

"The rest of them being...?"

"Followers of the Teacher."

"I'm not," she says.

"Of course, that's something you'd be trained to say."

Amalin pauses and thinks.

"What information could I get out of you?"

Madison goes silent.

"Let me rephrase that. Whatever information you think they want to tease out of you, I don't want it."

"I don't *think* they want it. I *know* they do."

"That's not what I meant. I'm talking as I'm going here. Sorry. Look, I don't want to play mind games. I just want out of here."

"Then why do you keep asking me if I was an artist?"

Amalin points to The Thunderbird on the wall.

Madison rolls her eyes.

"Really?"

Amalin rubs her eyes.

"I don't know. I liked stuff like that when I was younger. I used to live with a bunch of cool people like you. Artists. Comedians. I lived in this rented house in Atlanta for a long time. And ... I wanted to write at one point. I wanted to write actually. I read a lot, like a whole lot. But by the time I started to try to write, there weren't any more publishers, people didn't watch streaming or TV like they used to, they stopped using the internet, they stopped reading, everything got crazy before the bottom fell out. Nobody was going to read my words. I didn't have any time. I had to fend for myself. Who the fuck was going to use precious resources to publish books?"

"What the fuck does that have to do with me?"

"I just wanted to know someone who got to do that kind of work, follow the dream before it all fell apart."

Madison turned in her cot.

"Well, I didn't," she says. "And I didn't know anyone who did."

"I'm not a plant," Amalin says.

"I believe you a little more now."

"Good," she says and turns around to fall asleep.

"But what if that thing I know, the reason I'm down here, can help you get out of this çell and get close enough to the Teacher to kill him?"

Amalin opens her eyes.

27

In the morning, the guards open the steel door and lead them out of the cell. They don't bother to tie their wrists or cover their eyes, pushing them forward instead with their high-caliber, semi-automatic rifles. Amalin feels the barrel against her shoulder blade. She tries to swivel her neck to get a better look at the guards; three guards to move two unnamed prisoners. There's no shortage of men here. She studies their eyes: two brown, one blue. Their faces are obscured by red bandanas. They lead them through the archway to a brick alcove where water drizzles from a copper cylinder in the wall. The blue-eyed boy hands Amalin a bar of handmade soap. Another gives Madison a razor and a detached rear-view mirror as she takes off her clothes. The blue-eyed guard snaps his fingers at Amalin and points to Madison's pile of clothes on the floor.

"You don't have all day. Clean yourself."

Madison drinks a few handfuls of water from the pipe.

Amalin takes off her clothes, hiding the knife in her boot by bunching her pant legs over the laces.

"Faster," he says.

She finishes undressing and stands under the trickle of frigid water. Her skin tightens as she splashes herself and wets her hair.

The guards keep their rifles pointed at them, staring at them through their sights.

"Aren't you supposed to keep those at your side unless you intend to shoot?"

"Shut up."

She lathers the soap and rubs it across her chest. Madison uses the same lather to shave her face and legs.

"Alright, that's enough. You're clean."

He tosses them a single towel.

Madison sets her hand on Amalin's shoulder.

"You need to drink."

Amalin nods and returns to the copper tube. She drinks all she can stand until her stomach feels cold and distended.

"That's enough."

They put on their clothes and shuffle toward the archway.

*   *   *

Madison traces the edge of the Thunderbird's wing as the light fades.

"Do I look like a girl to you?"

Amalin shifts onto her side. The metal frame of the cot creaks.

"No, not really. A little more now that you're shaved. But you don't look like a man either. You're just you. I don't know how else to put it."

Madison says nothing and rests her hands on her chest.

They both lie, staring up toward the ceiling, in silence. The light fades. Madison doesn't start the pressure lamp.

Amalin listens to her breath in the crowding dark.

"It was the one with blue eyes," Madison says.

"I don't want to hear about it."

"He looked at you today."

"All three of them were looking at us."

"He'll start to come by more and more until he takes you to the showers by himself. He makes sure no one else is coming by forcing you to stick your head around the corner to listen for footsteps."

"I said I don't want to hear about it."

"I'm trying to help you. That's the only time he sets his gun to the side, the only time one of them is alone."

Amalin lifts her arm above her head. She feels Madison lie next to her in the cot, pulling her free arm across her shoulders.

"What are you doing?"

"Just hold me, please," Madison says.

Amalin wraps her arms around her. She feels her breathing against her.

"You said we would have been friends. Did you mean that?"

"I did," Amalin says.

28

When she wakes up, her arms are empty. She looks over the edge of the cot to see Madison on the stone floor in a pool of blood. Her throat is slashed, the neck still spurting. She gargles as she unconsciously fights for air, still holding Amalin's knife. Blood wells up in her mouth, spilling across her chin, filling the gaps in her teeth. Amalin watches, paralyzed, as her gut heaves and shudders. Her head falls to the side, eyes still open as if trained on something, pensive. Amalin watches her for another minute before realizing she's dead. She reaches down and takes the knife from her limp grasp and replaces it with the toothbrush handle.

She sidesteps the pool of blood and pounds her fist on the steel door, yelling for help. No one comes. She slides her back down the door. The light catches the Thunderbird while Madison's body lies in shadow.

Her hands tremble as she takes in a breath. The backs of her knees are pressed against her buttocks as she sits against the door. Her heart races. Her knees are weak. Her veins pulse as if clogged with molasses.

She remembers her warmth, the sisterly nuzzle of her chin against the crook of her shoulder.

She pounds her fist against the door again.

Madison's body starts to stink. Amalin covers her face with her shirt. She notices the book underneath Madison's cot beside the kerosene can and picks it up before the blood reaches it. The spine is stiff and the pages are crisp. Madison hadn't read at a single page. Amalin tries to read it, but she doesn't understand it: some kind of modern philosophical thesis. She doesn't like the voice in the first two pages. It probably didn't matter what kind of book it was; she thinks. It was probably given to her as toilet paper, though, she hadn't torn out a single page either. It was the most pristine book she had seen in years. Was this a form of re-education given by the Teacher?

She tosses the book to the side.

The day continues and, still, no one comes.

Madison's blood dries and fuses the corpse to the floor. The smell is so putrid. She lays herself face down on the floor and sucks air through the meal slot at the base of the door. She falls asleep with her mouth pressed against the steel.

29

She wakes as they shove a worn plate of meat and potatoes in her face. She reaches her hand through the slot and grabs the guard's boot. He stomps on her fingers to keep her away.

"My cellmate is dead!"

He says nothing and steps back.

"Don't you walk away. There's a rotting corpse in here."

He pauses and then speaks.

"Why'd you kill your cellmate?"

"She killed herself."

"Name?"

"Madison."

"The new one?"

"No, she was already here."

"The man?"

"Oh, godammit. Yes, her. You know who I'm talking about. Goddammit!"

He pounds the stock of his rifle against the steel.

"Stop swearing," he says. "Just hold on. We'll get someone to take out the body."

"No, you need to get me out of here first."

"Not a chance."

"Listen!" she says. "Listen to me. She's-"

"He!" he says, correcting her.

"I'm the last person alive who knows where the schematic is buried. She told me."

He hesitates, thinking to himself.

"Tell us where it is."

"No," she says. "I want an audience with the Teacher. I want to state my case as to what happened and I want to tell him where it is myself."

"I can't do that."

"I know you can't. Get someone who can. Those are my terms. Does the Teacher want clean water or does he want to wait around for typhoid to kill everyone here?"

She hears the guard's footsteps as he walks away.

*   *

Four guards return and open the steel door. They bind Amalin's wrists and throw a pillowcase over her head. She doesn't bother to ask where they're headed, moving forward at the prompting of the rifle barrel in her shoulder blade. She thinks she can hear them hang behind to drag Madison's body across the stone floor.

"Turn left."

She recognizes the blue-eyed boy's voice, the cadence of false authority. The air turns hot. Sunshine pierces the seams of the pillow case. Dust fills her nostrils. They push her further and she feels soft ground beneath her feet. The sunshine abruptly dies, the cloth around her face overcome by sudden shade. They've entered an echoing vestibule.

"Stop here. Give me your hands."

She separates her bound hands from her back. They cut her free. A wooden door closes behind her. She inches forward and feels the first step a creaking wooden staircase on her boot and tears off the pillow case. She stands at the base of a narrow brick tower. The steps wind upward. She looks back. She's alone.

30

Amalin climbs the stairwell. The wooden steps creak and give under her minimal weight. The wind blows stray flecks of dust and grit through a small open window where she can see part of the wall enclosing the ramshackle town. She enters an open study, a workspace, and a personal library. There are three desks positioned at oblique angles across two enormous rugs opposite a glass-encased bookshelf that covers the entirety of the far wall. Another breeze passes through the room, flapping the pages of open books and half-spread maps weighed down with brass trinkets and antique tools, compasses, mementos, and the like. The shutterless windows look medieval, the shape of Asturian alcoves.

A tall, slim man with curly, graying hair and a short beard steps toward her from the edge of the bookshelf as he shuts a thick leather-bound volume with one hand like a sprung animal trap. He wears a jet-black priest's cassock void of a clerical collar and carries a silver-plated conversion pistol, a Colt Dragoon, on a bandolier belt.

"I understand you have information for me."

"As a matter of fact," she says. "What happened to your guard outside the wall, that was a misunderstanding."

"Was it? You killed a good man. He was a boy really, seventeen. Begged his father to let him take on the responsibility. He passed all the tests, proved he was a good soldier. But still, I wouldn't let him guard without his father's consent. I have to answer to his father now, explain that you killed him because of a... misunderstanding."

"I didn't kill him."

"Who then?"

"The boy, my boy."

"The Mexican? He's your son?"

"That's not what I meant. He's not my son. I found him out in the desert. He used to live here with his parents. They were killed on an excursion for food. I was returning him to the village."

"The village? Is that what they're calling us?"

"I don't know how else to put it."

The Teacher rubs his nose.

"This haven is called Alberta City. I grew up in Canada. I thought it had a nice sound to it. Where are you originally from? Mexico? Honduras?"

"Santa Fe originally," she says. "But I lived most of my life on the east coast. Georgia."

"Savannah?"

"Atlanta."

"But you still ended up beyond The Cordon after all."

She sighs.

"Yeah."

"How did that come about?"

"That's not what I'm here to talk to you about," she says.

"You're only here because I allowed you here, not because of your bargaining chip. I can put you right back into that hole and starve you to death in your cell if I want. Why did you shoot my guard?"

"I told you. I didn't shoot him. Neither did the trucker."

"The black gentleman?"

"Yeah."

"The boy really shot him?"

She nods.

"We were only talking. He was about to take the boy back into the city."

"To repatriate?"

"That's how they said it. But he's confused. He hasn't learned English well enough yet and he thought...he thought he was going to shoot us. It happened fast. We gave ourselves up after it happened."

The Teacher steps over to the far desk and takes out two crystal glasses and the bottle of tequila she had stashed in the truck cabin.

"Drink?"

"I'd rather have water," she says.

"That's what we're here to discuss then, isn't it? Everyone would rather have water. Clean water. And you'd be the one to give it to us. Frank was one of my best innovators. He was a neo-liberal, tyrannical, Marxist, fascist, sexual deviant, you name it. He was a problem. But he had the best and most pragmatic ideas when it came to building this place up. He had the schematic for an updated water filtration system, something we can actually build with the limited resources we have."

"Who the fuck is Frank?"

"The cellmate you killed. Did he make you call him Madison? Ridiculous."

He pours the tequila and hands Amalin the glass before taking a seat in the leather chair by the desk.

"I didn't kill her."

"Him."

"I didn't kill anyone."

"And yet wherever you are, someone ends up dead. Am I supposed to believe it's just bad luck?"

"Yes."

He swallows the tequila.

They stare at one another.

"Where is the schematic?"

"Where is my partner?"

"Your partner? The black boy is your husband, your lover?"

"Partner," she says. "Like a law firm. We work together."

"When you grew up in what used to be the U.S., did you ever take much philosophy?"

"No."

"Or more importantly, did you understand the significance of living in The West."

"I didn't live in New Mexico very long."

"No, no. Not the western United States. The West. The Western world."

"What is the significance of the Western world?"

He sets the crystal glass down.

"It's everything. It's literally everything. The Western world, Western philosophy, is the difference between a city like this one with laws and codes, people living in harmony and working together, and everything else out there past those walls where it's kill or be killed, where resources are taken up the second they're usurped, where the weak are exploited and destroyed, no justice, no light, no love. That's what The West is."

He points to the books behind the glass.

"Socrates. Descartes. Christianity. Is that what you're getting at?"

"Exactly. You're smarter than you let on. You have this aura of intensity around you, but I can see it's a sham. You're as lost as anyone."

"What does this have to do with anything?"

"It has everything to do with everything. You and I. Your partner. The boy."

"Then explain."

"I am," he says. "Western Civilization is the most important cultural force ever produced by humanity and it's going to save the world we live in again as it has in the past. I've spent my entire life explaining that solid fact in the teachings. The people who live here, they understand this. But as you can see, we're the last bastion of the West. Alberta City is all we have left. If it goes then we have nothing left, no hope. This place is fragile. It's a powder keg and I have to constantly stamp out the fuse and show the people that these ideals are worth preserving. But people are desperate and they can't just take my word for it. I have to show them something. They have to see the benefits for themselves. Water, food, shelter, order."

She says nothing and thinks about the knife in her boot.

He scratches his chin and stares into her eyes.

"Are you familiar with the utilitarian perspective? Or the good-fruit analogy?"

She shakes her head.

"If an action bears good fruit, is it justified? You pick an apple off the tree and feed yourself and your family, but something or someone had to die for that soil to be enriched."

He stands up from the chair and slowly steps toward the window.

"Sacrifices have to be made to preserve something with this much fragility in its nature. The boy, the Mexican, he may be disturbed, it may have been an accident or a misunderstanding--"

"You killed him, didn't you?" she says tightening her grip on the glass. Her free hand becomes a fist.

The Teacher frowns.

"Of course not. He's a little boy. He's unaware of his actions. But the fact of the matter is, a guard was murdered at the gates of the city. Do you think these people here will take in a child with open arms if he's a murderer? No. He needs care and education, therapy for his trauma. I can give that to him, but the people won't accept him if they know what he's done. Do you see? Someone must accept the responsibility. You have the location of the schematic. You have something to offer. But your partner…"

"What have you done with Isaiah?"

The Teacher points out the window, past the hay and adobe awning, to the open courtyard. The dust rises as the wind swells. He calls down to the guards. They bring a young man with a pillowcase over his head into the center of the courtyard. A small gathering of people stands in a shaded dugout to watch. The guards take him to the far wall and tie him to the wooden plank opposite a small firing squad.

"This is why I brought you here," The Teacher says. "You have to understand the sacrifice that has to be made. You have to understand why I have to give them someone. To promote order. To prevent bedlam. This is what it takes. Do you understand why it's right to give me the location of the schematic for the filter?"

She nods.

"I understand. I understand everything."

He smiles and places his hand on her shoulder.

"I can give you some supplies and a few good men. Will you bring it back?"

"No," she says. "Madison told me about it, but she never told me where she hid it. I lied to get up here."

She breaks the glass against his face as he reaches for his pistol. The shards slice his cheek and the bridge of his nose. The liquor stings. She pushes his hand down and keeps him from drawing. With both his hands fighting to pull his gun from the holster, he steps back to create enough room to shoot, but she stays close, pushing him against the wall with her entire body, groining him as hard as she can. She finds a moment to free her right hand to pull the blade from her boot. The pistol discharges, narrowly missing his femoral artery and the side of her foot. She plunges the knife, stained with Madison's dried blood, deep into The Teacher's gut. He stares at the handle in his stomach and lets out a weak gasp. His hands fall to his side. She plucks the Colt from his holster and reloads the single cartridge from the bandolier on his waist and then rips the knife out at an angle to tear apart as much tissue as she can. He slides down the wall and crawls to the window, yelping for the guards. She sheathes the blade and sets the gun on the sill.

"What are you doing?"

She steps behind him and grips the back of his head and the contour of his chin. She hopes she can manage it on her first try.

"No, please--"

His ligaments stretch and pop.

He keeps on breathing.

She lifts his head again. It feels heavier this time.

His neck snaps with an audible crack.

She lets his limp skull slam into the hard floor.

She can hear the guards coming up the stairs and barricades the entrance with an upturned desk. Quickly, she fits the bandolier belt around her waist and props The Teacher's body against the window. She uses his arm like a short rope, dislocating it from the socket as she swings down and crashes through the awning into the courtyard amid an avalanche of red dust and flying hay. She races across the courtyard range toward Isaiah. Turning, she approaches the dugout where the congregation scatters in hysterics. A short man lifts a shotgun in her direction. She fires and he falls back. She grabs the pump-action shotgun and pulls the hammer back on the pistol. She presses the barrel between a young girl's eyes. The girl is paralyzed by fear.

"You come with me."

"Leave her alone," a young man yells at her from a distance.

She fires at him.

The bullet hits his shoulder. He collapses, shaking.

She presses the hot barrel against the young girl's neck, burning a red circle into her flesh. She screams. Amalin moves her from out of the dugout, toward Isaiah, using her as a human shield. The girl's presence doesn't stop the guards from shooting from the tower.

Amalin cuts Isaiah loose and rips the cloth off his head. His face is swollen beyond recognition. She thrusts the shotgun into his arms.

"Kill who you have to," she says.

He nods, exhausted.

They take cover behind the girl. A stray bullet shatters the top half of her hand. She drops, screaming, blood spurting from the wound.

Amalin and Isaiah race for the dugout trailed by a burst of semi-automatic fire. They enter a lightless, clay corridor and run until the sound of gunfire fades.

"Where are we going?" Isaiah manages to say between breaths.

"I don't know."

"How'd you get out?"

"I'll tell you later. Then I'll tell you how I killed The Teacher."

"You're serious?" he says. "We aren't gonna live to get out of here."

"Shut up."

The ground slopes upward and they can see the bright desert sky at the opposite end of the tunnel. Amalin checks the corner and signals for Isaiah.

31

Isaiah keeps the stock of the shotgun pressed against his shoulder, passing through the threshold into the light of the outdoor garage. He stops and stares at his truck. The tires of Isaiah's rig are chained to a row of cast-iron pillars, remnants of the old mill upon which the city was built. There's a fleet of Toyota pickups and a Humvee parked in the open ground gathering a thick layer of windblown dust.

"We need keys," she says.

"It's one road in and one road out. We won't make it."

Amalin spots a man in a green jumpsuit cowering behind one of the pillars. She pulls him out by the collar and crushes his nose with the butt of the pistol.

"You got a gun on you?"

He shakes his bloody face.

"Give us the keys to one of these trucks."

He points to a rack on the far wall from which the keys dangle.

"Which one's to which?"

"They numbered," he says. "There's a little number on the side of the hood."

"Lay on the ground. Close your eyes."

Isaiah grabs the keys to the closest pickup and tosses them to her. She unlocks the doors.

"How much gas is in these?"

The mechanic on the floor doesn't respond.

"Hey! How much gas is in these?"

Isaiah loads four gas cans into the truck bed.

"It doesn't fucking matter. I got it. Start the engine."

She sets the key in place and turns it. The truck engine rumbles. The dashboard lights up.

"Get in."

"Wait," he says lifting the fifth can. He turns to the man on the ground. "You got matches?"

"There's some in the red toolbox top shelf."

Isaiah grabs the box and shoves it into his upper pocket. He pours the gasoline over the other cars and creates a puddle beside the mechanic.

"Get out of here."

He forces himself to his feet, shaking, and runs from into the dark of the corridor.

Isaiah runs a trail of gas to the door of the truck.

Amalin watches as he gets inside and rolls down the window. He strikes a match and drops it. She shifts into drive.

"Stop," he says. "It went out."

She keeps her foot on the break.

He strikes two fresh matches and lets them burn before dropping them out the window. The flames rise along the edge of the truck.

"Go, go."

*   *   *

By the time the guards discover the truck speeding away from the walls of Alberta City, they're too far to shoot. She navigates the maze of rocks and stationary bulldozers and hits the highway. Isaiah leans back in his seat.

"They're unorganized," she says. "They're not professionals. That's why we got out."

"Neither are you," Isaiah says. "We acted fast and we got lucky."

She scoffs.

"I killed The Teacher and saved your life."

Her hands shake with excess adrenaline as she grips the steering wheel.

Isaiah closes his eyes.

"What happened to the kid?"

"I don't know. I don't care."

"I thought he was like a son to you."

"No," she says. "He was a means to an end. I don't care what happens to him now."

"Yeah, you do. You're not a killer."

She laughs.

"I am though."

He lays his head against the window.

"What now?"

"We get our money."

"And spend it on what?"

"You can get a new truck. I was saving up for a place to live in the militarized zone. South of the refugee slums."

Isaiah shakes his head in silence.

"What?"

He says nothing and counts the shells in the shotgun.

"How many you got?"

"Three."

"They didn't take out the plug?"

"Probably not. But I'm not about to chance it and open this sucker up to see."

"Better than one, I guess."

"Where'd you get that gaudy thing?" he says, pointing to the revolver and bandolier belt.

"The Teacher."

Isaiah looks at his swollen face, bruised face in the side mirror.

"I don't recognize myself."

"Did they break anything?"

"No. Not that I can feel. I think I have all my teeth still."

"You smell like feces," she says.

"I'd pay top-dollar for shower and a nurse right about now."

"Any water we find, we're drinking it."

"I know that. Don't forget I'm from here. You're the one from the outside The Cordon."

"Yeah, I thought you were from North Carolina."

"Why'd you think that?"

"You named your dog Winston-Salem."

"I saw it on cigarette packs and the side of a truck once when I saved him."

She nods.

"I see."

He thinks to himself in silence.

"They shot my dog," he says, in a matter-of-fact way.

"Better than having to eat him."

"What do you think they were feeding us in that prison?"

Amalin realizes the tough, gristle she and Madison had been eating was more than likely dog meat. Was it an insult or just pragmatism?

Isaiah falls asleep. She drives until sunset.

32

She parks near a cluster of dead trees and gets out of the truck. A vulture looks down at her, perched on the leafless top branch of the nearest ironwood. It spreads its wings and takes off into the darkening sky as she snaps off a few lower branches and carves away thin portions of dried-up bark. The tree shakes in the sudden absence of the carrion bird's weight.

Isaiah rolls down the passenger window and leans his head out the side.

"What are you doing?"

"I'm making a fire."

"So they can track us? Stop it."

He rolls up the window.

She realizes how foolish it would be to make a fire and kicks the small pile of wood across the ground. She returns to the truck and leans back in her seat.

"We'll die out here without food," she says. "I should have shot that buzzard when I saw it."

"That was a vulture, not a buzzard," Isaiah says with his eyes closed. "And you can't eat either. They're toxic."

"I think I knew that."

*　　　*　　　*

She wakes up with a gun under her chin, her body slanted half-way out the open door of the truck, caught in blinding unnatural light. A dark man with black gloves and a surgical mask over his face takes the silver revolver from her holster.

"I'm not gonna hurt you and you'll get your gun back. It's your property. I just don't want you to do anything stupid."

She looks over as a young woman, her face covered from the nose down by a fume respirator mask, holds a pistol to Isaiah's temple. She reaches into the truck with her free hand and takes the shotgun. She carries a long-range rifle in a makeshift sleeve on the side of her backpack.

"Hit the safety on that Mossberg. It's at the top there," he says to the woman.

They move them from the truck leaving the doors ajar and have them place their hands over the engine hood. Isaiah and Amalin interlock their fingers, holding one another, stretching their stomachs over the cold metal.

The man lowers the flashlight.

"Y'all coming from Alberta City?"

Amalin nods.

"I'm gonna guess just from the hue of your skin, you're not big fans of The Teacher. You don't have to answer that question, but you do look like you're running away from something and this is a stolen truck and these are stolen weapons. That's y'alls' business. The trouble is, you're knocking on the door to The Nation. Why is that?"

"I didn't know. We're just passing through. Found a place to stop."

"So, it's a bad coincidence, huh?"

"Yes."

"Ok. Well, just get the hell out of here and we shouldn't have any problems. We'll put the guns in the truck bed here while you drive off. Mosi here is gonna have a bead trained on ya until you're good and clear."

"Wait! We'll trade you a can of gasoline for some food and water."

She looks into the indigenous man's eyes and sees genuine pity.

He shakes his head.

"I'm sorry. I can't spare anything for you."

Mosi, the young woman, speaks through the respirator.

"Let's at least give'em a canteen."

"Alright," he concedes. "I'll put it in the back with your guns."

They escort them back into the truck. Amalin starts the engine.

Mosi holsters her pistol and bolts a round into the rifle.

The man kicks the bumper, signaling her. Amalin shifts into drive and rolls out of the tree patch, heading through the scrub brush.

33

Isaiah helps her drain the canteen dry. The water has a sweet flavor from the added electrolytes. He gives her the last sip.

"That's it," she says, holding the empty canteen.

"Yep, that's it."

"How many days will that keep us alive do you think?"

"Two. Maybe three."

34

They find their way back to the plains. Isaiah slows and parks the truck behind a hill near the highway. He rousts Amalin awake.

"You're turn to drive."

She wipes the crust from her eyes and slides over, taking Isaiah's place behind the wheel as he steps out to stretch his legs. He leans forward and touches his lower back.

The sun pierces the windshield, scorching the synthetic material of the dashboard.

Amalin watches him as he hoists one of the gasoline cans from the bed and fills the tank. She turns, looking toward the rolling hills in the shadow of the distant mountains, and sees the convoy approaching.

A gunshot sounds as the oncoming driver fires a pistol at the sky, a signal.

Isaiah steps in front of the truck still clutching the gas can. He looks back at Amalin. She lowers her head against the steering wheel and, without looking, draws The Teacher's pistol.

He turns back and tilts the can, spreading a line across the remnants of sun-bleached asphalt.

"Are they Nazis?" she calls out.

"Who cares what they are?" he says, striking a match.

The wall of flame rises and forms a barrier of black smoke.

Amalin kicks the door open and walks into the road. She hands Isaiah the shotgun.

He flicks the safety and pumps a shell into the chamber.

Amalin sets a cartridge between her teeth.

"We could still make a run for it," he says.

She catches a glimpse of the ethnostate flag through the smoke. The front hood of the Humvee is painted with the Dixie flag. A lone rider on a dirt bike cruises through fire. Isaiah blows him off his seat. The bike skids away. She fires a shot at the windshield. Six shots pelt the stationary truck behind them with a tin-like ring. She loads the cartridge from her teeth and thumbs back the hammer. She feels her gut untwist and her shoulder loosen.

"This is it," she says. "Thank God we didn't have to starve to death."

Isaiah ignores her and walks toward the dying flames.

She laughs, staring above his head.

"Can you see it?" she yells. "Do you see that in the sky? Can you see it? Do you see its wings?"

The plain-clothes soldier crests the hill and looks out at the wall of storage containers painted dark green and draped in camouflage nets. From the opposite peak, they appear as nothing more than a dip in the natural terrain. He walks past the stashed wellheads standing upright like a row of mechanical crosses and calls out to the crew in the earth-covered control bay. There's no one. A lunchbox sits in the rolling chair. A half-drunk cup of coffee rests on a metal shelf. He sets out toward the proppant containers and sees the blood splatter against the bright metal curvature of the tank. The body at his feet is nearly decapitated. He finds the rest of the crew strewn across the dust, vultures pecking at their bodies.

PART TWO:

The Durango Kid

PART TWO

The Durango Kid

1

Pancho steers his camel away from the dry arroyo at the first sign of rain and lets it amble along at its own pace once they reach the high plateau. His guide, the one that left him at the edge of Bunker Town, had told him about a small settlement north of the canyon called Techo. After the sun dies and the clouds block out the stars overhead, the rain falls hard and straight, clearing the tracks he had been following for the last three days. He passes the afore-mentioned canyon and, in the valley below the regenerating chaparral, sees the first few metal shacks and rain-soaked tents of Techo. He wonders why a settlement nestled so low in the valley would call itself Techo when the more apt description of the terrain is *"suelo."* The thought fades from his mind as he searches for the safest route into town. He signals for the hybrid beast to fold itself onto the rain-slick grit for him to dismount and cover the valuable saddle which carries his worldly possessions with a waterproof tarp. Taking the reins, he leads the bear-colored creature into town. An old woman wrapped in Mexican blanket peers out from a scrap-metal eave and calls out to him.

"Spanish or English?"

"Whichever," he says.

She shines a light at him.

"You looking to put that camel up for the night?"

"Get it out of the rain, yes," he says, trying to show her a smile through his thick beard, squinting in the light.

"There's a stable two doors down on the left. One stall is still free. But you're sleeping on the hay. We don't have any beds to spare. Seems like everybody's passing through tonight."

"I'd rather sleep on the hay anyway. Keeps this one calm," he says, stroking the camel's soaked fur. "Plus it keeps me closer to my things."

"Well, you have a good night then."

"My partner hasn't already gotten here, has he?"

"Well, who is he?"

"'Bout this tall. Grey coat. Blue pants. Lopsided black hat. Russian accent. Blonde. Scars all over his face."

"Yeah, he's up at the Robuck's tent with some others. Asked about buying camels."

Pancho tips his hat to her.

"Good to hear he made it okay. Thank you very much, Ma'am"

"You keep to yourself; you hear?"

"I always do," he says leading the camel through the ankle-deep muck.

He enters the dark stable where three alpacas and two Arabian camels lounge and chew at the piled Bermuda hay. He leads his hybrid into the last available stall and unstraps the reins but leaves the saddle. He drapes the reins over a nearby support beam. The rain pelts the tin roof. He stomps the mud from his boots and drags the rain barrel from outside the padlocked back door to the stall. He unscrews the mesh-filter top and drinks a few handfuls before his camel cranes its neck down and commences drinking. He rests his hand atop the 1911 on his gun belt and stares at the other animals. When the camel is finished eating and drinking, he rests alongside it in the stall, setting a small digital timer for three hours. When he wakes up, the rain is still falling, albeit softer. He allows the camel to keep resting. He brushes the hay off his back and walks into town looking for the tent.

2

He finds a green tent beside an old airstream trailer and stands behind the plywood barrier to watch the entrance. A coyote yaps in the distance through the diminishing rain. Strange, he thinks. He watches the entrance for some time and determines no one to be watching out. He draws his pistol and chambers a cartridge. Peeling back the tent flap, he enters the musty cavern. The smell of unwashed men and stale hemp and tobacco fills his nostrils. Seven unrelated travelers all sleep on thin mattresses splayed across the mucky earth separated by wood crates and half-melted plastic buckets upturned like miniature tables in the chaos. Unlit pressure lamps and now-dead solar chargers, empty bottles of liquor, empty growlers of rice and millet beer, fill in the blank spaces between each hard-spring, salvaged mattress. Some of them snore. Others unconsciously suck at the air as they dream of Two-Spirit and Thai kathoey prostitutes. He finds Vasily near the back entrance. He holsters the pistol and nudges him awake, offering him a cigarette from the stainless-steel case.

"*Hola. Que pasa,* my friend," the Russian says, waking to Pancho's face.

"Not much," he says. "Smoke?"

"Yeah," he says, taking a fresh smoke from the case. He leans forward to suck the flame from Pancho's flint and rope wick lighter.

"Fancy seeing you."

"Quiet, you know. Everyone here sleeps."

"No problem."

"How did you find me?"

"Looking for a bed. Just got lucky, I guess."

"Yes, yes. Хорошо. We have no more beds though."

"I can see it. What's with you? Where are you headed?"

"I go to Mexico."

"Mexico? Why you goin' to Mexico."

Vasily sucks on the cigarette.

"Eh, the damn Chinese. They want me...Hey, you know, I didn't want to leave you back in Bears Ears, but..."

"Forget it. That's in the past. Everyone had to run for it. The whole thing fell apart."

"We didn't even get our money when we got back to the outpost," he whispers. "Those cheap sons of bitches."

Pancho smiles with Vasily.

"They were cheap. That they were, my friend."

"It is good to see you, but it is maybe not so safe, you know?"

"How come you say that?"

He leans forward to further lower his voice.

"Past twelve miles, you know, I am being followed."

"The Chinese?"

"They hire a bounty hunter, a tracker after me."

"How do you know?"

"I can tell," he says, tapping the ash on the ground. "There's always someone after me."

"You seen 'em?"

He shakes his head.

"I double back one night and see camel tracks, But I can't find his camp. So I head for arroyo. Maybe I drowned him when the rain came, or at least my tracks are now gone. Always one step ahead."

Pancho smiles.

"Smart man."

"So how about you. What do you do now?"

"I'm lookin' for work. Just moving around."

"Hey, you take me to Mexico and I pay you there."

He nods his head.

"Yeah, that seems like a good plan. But you still owe me from Bears Ears."

"I pay you for Bears Ears and Mexico. How about it?"

Pancho offers him his hand.

"Come outside and we'll get going. Get ahead of the tracker."

"It's raining. He won't find me. We leave in the morning."

"You got yourself a deal, Vasily."

He shakes his hand firmly, smiling.

Pancho pulls his arm toward him and presses the pistol against his chest. The gunshot resonates through the tent. Blood peppers the pillow and mattress. Vasily's shirt catches fire from the muzzle flash.

Another man reaches for a cheap Glock from under a bucket.

Pancho shoots for the gun from the man's hand.

A young man to his right manages to fire a shot past his head, piercing the tent.

Pancho shoots him dead.

"Does anyone else want to die?"

The five travelers raise their empty hands.

"I'm gonna drag this man's body through the mud. Anyone leaves this tent or tries to stop me will die. I don't have to prove what kind of shot I am. Now, go back to sleep."

He grabs Vasily by one leg and drags his body off the mattress.

He rides with the corpse draped over the back of the saddle, wrapped in a blanket and duct-taped on both ends to seal off as much of the smell as possible. He returns through the savage hills and rocky canyons to the salt flats where the desert is its mirror image of the far-off horizon and traces back through the ubiquity of the landscape until he finds the Chinese People's Liberation Army base named for Commander Liang Yang.

A lone soldier lounges at the outermost checkpoint gate beneath his umbrella. He looks out at the approaching camel through his sunglasses. His face is streaked with white swathes of sunscreen.

Pancho recognizes him.

"Bo, what's up?"

The soldier adjusts his floppy hat.

"Pancho?"

"Yeah."

"Alright," he says, preemptively buzzing open the first automatic gate.

The camel takes its time reaching the loading dock and Pancho dismounts onto the searing hot steel platform.

"Who do you got for us?" Bo says in an American accent.

"The Russian. Vasily Predag."

"No, shit? Sneaky bastard."

"Not anymore."

"Fuck you, Ruski," he says and spits on the wrapped blanket.

"How's it been?"

"How do you think it's been? It's too hot to fuckin' think."

"Well, tell your guys to hurry it up. This piece of shit's been emulsifying on my saddle for a day."

"You got a rifle on that saddle?"

"Not anymore."

Pancho unhooks the long, Velcro-flap holster from the saddle and hands it to Bo.

"Semi-Auto Benelli."

"What?"

"It's a fuckin' shotgun," he says, unhooking his gun belt. He hands it the 1911 and three spare, eight-shot magazines over and Bo locks the weapons away in the kiosk. He closes the outer gate and opens the next checkpoint as another soldier takes the reins and leads the camel to a shaded corridor within the frame of the safety wall.

Pancho calls out to the man.

"Hey, don't bother putting the saddle back on once you take it off. You assholes always fuck up the girth and you screw up my camel's hip bones."

"We'll take good care of her," the soldier yells in a thick, Sichuan Hua accent. "What's her name?"

"It's a camel," he mumbles to himself. "Camels don't have names."

4

Pancho is allowed a shower and a chance to clean his clothes before meeting the *shaojiang* to see about his payment.

He steps inside the wood-paneled building and sits down in a lobby across from the assistant's desk.

The tinted glass door opens. Choi, the *shaojiang*, is dressed down wearing a white shirt with a Western bolo tie. He grins from ear to ear.

"Pancho! Get your ass in here."

Pancho stands up and approaches the young assistant's desk.

"You got keys to the armory?"

"What?"

"Keys to the armory. You got armory privileges?"

"Yeah," the assistant says, looking confused.

Pancho lays down a 45 ACP cartridge and rifled slug shell on the desk.

"Go get me a box of each one of them."

The assistant looks at Choi for approval.

Choi nods.

He gets up and walks past them as they enter the small office.

"Positive I.D. came back just now on Predrag. Good work."

"I didn't shoot him in the face," he says, taking a seat.

Choi laughs. He sets his hand on the dial to the safe and spins the combination. He counts the money out on the desk in front of Pancho and stuffs the bills into a sand and waterproof vinyl envelope. Pancho packs it into his boot.

"I was gonna try this new whiskey, just came in. Care for a shot?"

"Please. You mind if I smoke?"

"Light up."

Pancho lights a stick of hemp and exhales a pungent fog over the desk. Choi hands him a glass of Single Malt and they toast. He sips the liquor.

"That's good."

"It's good to have friends in high places."

Pancho nods and takes a puff.

"You staying the night?"

"If I can help it."

"What's next?"

He shrugs.

"I might go back to Bunker Town. See about building a house."

"I could use your help on another job."

"I don't know. I was thinking about going up north. See what it's like."

"When kings lose their direction, they become servants," Choi says.

"I'm already a servant."

"No, you're a professional."

"Who else do you want dead?"

"It's a little more delicate than that. This one is more of a favor."

"I don't do favors."

"You're not doing me a favor. I'm doing someone a favor. But you'll be the one I'm paying."

Pancho swigs the remainder of the whiskey.

"Who's the favor for?"

Choi swirls the liquid in his glass.

"You ever been to the plains?"

"Once," he says. "As a child. Isn't that where the Nazis used to live?"

"There haven't been any Nazis out there for twenty years. But I'll tell you what *is* out there, natural gas."

"I thought the Chinese military was here for a peace-keeping mission? A neutral power providing aid?" Pancho says, smiling

"Of course," Choi says.

"What's the angle?"

"Let's say there might be a hidden drill site that we don't know about."

"Okay."

"And no one knows about it either. Even if they found it, that's not a Chinese government site. It's some company. Who cares?"

"Who would know?"

"Exactly. But someone does know about it. The drilling for the hydraulic fracturing has been done. It's ready to pump in the fluid, but everyone who goes out to work on the site gets killed."

"It'd be better if they were gone."

"It'd be better for everyone."

The assistant walks into the office with a box of shells and cartridges.

"Leave 'em on the table," Choi says.

The assistant walks out in silence, closing the door behind him.

"They're sitting on a pile of bodies as we speak."

"I don't know," Pancho says. "Sounds like walking into an ambush."

"I could give you men."

"No, I work alone."

He thinks for a moment.

Choi drinks and sits down in his leather chair.

"You got the gray wolf's ghost."

"What?"

"In China, people venerate their ancestors during holidays and religious ceremonies and things. Hell, so do Mexicans. The Day of the Dead."

Pancho taps his ash on the floor.

"I don't know anything about that. Far as I can remember, I've lived in this shithole."

"Who raised you?"

"A mean old lady with one hand out by Alberta City, what was left of it. I didn't stay long."

"Who taught you to shoot?"

"I always knew how to shoot."

"Who taught you how to read and write and count?"

"The lady with a hook for a hand. Taught me English too."

"Your mother?"

"No. She was white."

"She took you in, huh?"

"For a time."

"See what I mean? The gray wolf's ghost."

Choi raises his glass and finishes the whiskey.

Pancho clicks his tongue and glances at the open safe.

"So who is it? Who's doing the killing?"

Choi leans back and clasps his hands.

"Might be the Nation. Osage-Cherokee alliance. Diné, possibly."

"But who's pulling the trigger? Six, seven men? Thirty?"

"That's why it's a favor, Pancho. It's the lieutenant at the Wan Shui outpost who asked me to send my best. He's got the details."

"That outpost was decommissioned," Pancho says.

"Officially, yes."

Pancho sighs and squashes his cigarette on the floor.

"Fuck it."

5

He stays on base overnight, lying half-awake in his hotel bed sucking at the grit between his teeth, thinking about the value of sudden death, the blessing of a bullet. In the morning, he has eggs and toast and broccoli for breakfast along with a liter of filtered water and five cups of black tea. He returns to the stable and pulls the ticket for his weapons. He sets and tightens the girths of the camel saddle himself and rides out just before noon.

The sun beats down on the flat earth. The ice in his canteens melts within minutes. He drinks one almost empty just to taste cold water for the last time. He stops the camel after a few miles to urinate and watches the yellow puddle between his legs begin to evaporate.

They travel north. With the sun setting behind him, he lays out a few Mexican blankets across harsh salt and opens the plastic bucket full of water and nopal patties for the camel. He rests on his bedroll in the fierce cold. At night, he wakes periodically in violent hypnic jerks, drawing his pistol from muscle memory alone. He dreams about thieves stealing his camel and feels their windpipes collapse in his strained hands once he catches them.

He wakes before sunrise and discards the empty bucket. The sky turns the color of smoke as clouds gather above him. He finds an echoing canyon in the afternoon and keeps the camel moving toward the high ground. He finds a steep slope out from the bottoms and rubs the camel's neck.

"You think you can manage?"

The camel stares into oblivion.

"No," he says to himself.

Fearful of the gathering cloud cover, he keeps the camel moving as fast as possible through the rocks. The crevice becomes shallow and he's able to escape on a long dune of salt and sand. From there, he reaches the high ground on a series of smooth rock formations above the desolation. An immense wall of petrified loam blocks his view of the east. The camel slows, strutting on its staff-like limbs.

A lone Joshua tree, alive, stands in the center of the tilted plateau like a monument.

He stares out beyond the gnarled limbs and sees a man walking toward the camel. He staggers along with his legs spread wide.

Pancho pulls open the Velcro flap of the shotgun case and retracts the bolt to chamber a slug. He rests the stock on his hip and flattens his finger on the trigger.

The man comes forward, undeterred by the shotgun. His eyes don't squint in the wind. He looks dazed, either drunk or heat-stricken. He staggers close enough for Pancho to finally see the buck knife handle sticking from his chest. A thin rivulet of blood trickles down his white shirt.

"You got yourself a souvenir?" he says.

The man stares at him and reaches into his pocket.

Pancho aims the shotgun.

"Not so fast."

The man pulls out a dollar bill.

"Pay for one of them canteens?" he says in a dry voice.

"Who stabbed you?" Pancho says.

"A group of drifters up yonder."

"What'd they look like?"

"Three men, one lady. White scarves on her face to keep from the dust. They took my water and camels. Got a camp on the other end of that rock."

"Good."

He waves the dollar bill.

"'Bout that canteen?"

"What about that canteen, old man? You don't waste water on a dead man in the desert."

Pancho flicks the safety on the shotgun and holsters it.

The old man falls to his knees.

"If you gonna kill them up there, the least you could do is get me my camels."

"If I end up killing them, you can get your own damn camel's back," Pancho says, riding away.

The old man collapses onto the ground, lying on his side.

Pancho looks back. He signals the camel to circle around. He returns to the man whose lips are red from having coughed up a portion of blood. By the time he reaches for a canteen, he realizes the old man is dead. The heat will dehydrate his body before the vultures can find it and his skin will mummify and peel off like dust and then the sun will bleach his bones.

He lets the camel rest in the shade below a tall rock while he scans the terrain with his binoculars. He doesn't see any indication of a camp and he isn't sure it's worth the risk. He searches for a path to circumvent the distant rock. The clouds overhead dissipate and the sun shines down as the temperature rises. He looks for markers to remember as he plans his evasive route. The wind picks up. The camel grunts. He climbs down from the rock and calms it before mounting the saddle. It lifts him back into the air. They continue, moving at a steady pace, veering off to the west.

He mumbles to himself in Spanish, recalling a fragment of an experience that might pass for the beginnings of a story. He mumbles and half-sings and sneers in the hot winds. The camel grunts again and he calms it, stroking the shaggy fur atop its head. The beast twists its neck to stare into his eyes, yelling with its wide mouth agape. He lifts himself from his heat-induced daydream. He acts normal and does what he can to calm the spooked camel, scanning the terrain for possible hiding spots. He can feel their eyes on him now. He races behind a blood-red rock and dismounts, tethering the reins to a dead acacia stump. The camel pulls at the dried wood, bleating. He leans against the rock with the shotgun stock against his shoulder and spits in the silence.

The sand shifts at his feet and kicks up in the wind as two men, faces obscured by white bandanas, rise from underneath a camouflage tarp spread across the loose ground. He whips around with the shotgun. His attacker grabs the barrel and raises it above his head as the shell discharges. He reaches under the stock with a hook-shaped blade and slashes at his stomach.

The second man takes a long bowie knife and cuts the camel's tethered reins.

Pancho averts the blade and draws his sidearm, killing the first thief. He holsters the 1911 and fires a rifled slug from the shotgun through the camel thief's chest. The shaggy hybrid shakes off the dead man's body.

A Winchester shot scars the rock beside him, glancing sideways.

Pancho sees the shooter on the high patch of dried earth, close to twenty yards off. He fires as he closes in on him. The shooter takes cover.

"Come on!" Pancho yells. "Come on, shoot me!"

He keeps his sites on the perch and steps back, whistling for his camel.

The shooter doesn't reemerge.

Pancho fires a warning shot and reloads the shotgun from the saddle. The camel bleats and runs its lips along his shoulder.

"There's still two more of these fuckers."

He looks at the sliced reins hanging off the creature's face.

"Fuck!"

A bullet whizzes past the camel's ear. A woman stands on the opposite end of the red rock with a revolver in her hand. Pancho fires a barrage of slugs and buckshot. She fires back, never once hitting him.

Holding extra rounds in the spaces between his fingers and one in his teeth like a massive cigar, he moves toward the rock and reloads after each shot. He turns the corner and spits the last round into his palm.

The woman is wounded and drags herself across the burning ground. She moves to reload the pistol, but her bloodied, tremoring hands keep dropping the loose cartridges.

Pancho kicks the gun aside and she gives up, splaying across the sand. He places his boot on her throat and calls out to the shooter on the perch.

She gargles and grasps at his heel.

"Come on! She's dying. Take a shot!"

He slams the shell into the loading port and aims.

The woman beneath him fights to free herself from under Pancho's boot as she chokes. He presses down harder as he focuses on the distant shooter. Her throat produces a cracking sound and her bloodshot eyes bulge. She reaches wildly, clawing at his leg.

The shooter's head emerges.

Pancho takes the shot.

The shooter slumps forward. His rifle slips from his hands.

Pancho lowers his shotgun.

The woman's hands fall back. Her legs quiver.

He lifts his boot and stomps down with his heel until her skull cracks and blood pools across the sand.

7

A town appears on the horizon; built on the slanted edge of a mountain like a growth of moss. The lights of distant houses and burning fires pull the stars closer to the earth. He rides out toward the settlement and knocks on the front door to the home annexed to the stable.

An old Mexican man with a graying mustache pushes the door open with the barrel of a sawed-off shotgun.

Pancho shows him his empty hands and speaks Spanish.

"I want to put my camel up for the night. How much?"

"Sixty dollars."

"Permit me to get it out of my boot?"

"Go ahead."

The old man gestures by waving the shotgun.

"I like shotguns too," Pancho says, pulling out the money. "Especially the kind without a pump."

"It's a piece of shit. You get two shots."

"Not if it's automatic," he says and hands the money to the old man.

The old man reaches out and takes the money. He doesn't lower the shotgun. His caution has probably kept him alive all these years.

"Follow me," he says.

He leads Pancho to the stables and fills his camel's stall with Bermuda hay and pours more water from a bucket into the aluminum trough.

"You got anything to eat?" he asks the old man.

"No," he says, shaking his head. "There's a place in the center of town, but you'll have to pay more money."

He finishes getting the camel situated and leaves it to walk through the shanty town. There isn't much to see and he isn't sure which place the old man meant but he finds an open-air kitchen just the same where he pays for a plate of seared peppers and braised camel meat. He wanders around for another half hour before finding a secluded patch of flowering cactus and sits on the dirt to admire the yellow color in the flickering firelight. A girl, half-draped in a threadbare dishabille, steps out from a lopsided camper with a bottle of Bourbon and an iron cup. She takes a seat beside Pancho and presumptuously caresses the small of his back. He breaks his gaze to look at her, telling her to stop with his eyes.

"You want a drink?" she says. "Three bucks."

He slips her the money and she pours the drink.

"Where are you from?"

"Not here," he says and takes a swig.

"Me neither. Can you read?"

He nods.

She shoves the bottle in his face and points to the label.

"What's that say?"

He pushes the bottle away from his face and focuses on the letters.

"Four Roses," he says.

"So just the picture then?"

He nods.

"You ever seen a rose before?"

"Nope."

"It kind of makes you think. How do we know what they are?"

"Words and thoughts are different than what's right in front of you. It's two separate worlds. You just pick things up."

"Yeah?"

"Sure," he says, feeling obligated to engage after having bought a drink from her.

She tilts the bottle and takes a swig.

"This stuff makes you sick if you drink more than a little," he says.

"I know it."

He stares at her bosom in the dim light.

"Can I touch it?"

"As long as you don't scratch it or pull on it."

"I'm not gonna do that."

"A lot of men do."

He sets his hand under her breast and feels its weight on his open palm.

"You're a killer, aren't you? That's why you got a gun belt."

"A lot of people carry guns that aren't killers."

"Maybe," she says, plunging the cork back into the bottle.

He reaches between her legs to feel the hair above her vulva.

"Careful," she says "I'm not sure if I'm done bleeding."

"I wouldn't have gotten this far in life if I was afraid of blood."

She leans back and closes her eyes.

"You talk like you're smart. You go to a school?"

"Something like that."

He holds the skin on both sides of her clit and rubs back and forth before gently pulling back the hood and lightly circling it with the tip of his middle finger. A piscine odor rises from her crotch.

"Stick it inside me."

He pushes his fingers inside her.

"No, stick your penis in me."

"You don't want to have to feed a child out here."

"I'm still bleeding a little bit. It won't happen."

He pulls his hand free and shows her the lack of blood on his fingers.

She pulls his hand in close and licks the fluid from his knuckles.

"Let me put you in my mouth then," she says.

"No," he says. "The last girl bit me and tried to take my gun."

"I won't bite you."

"I know you won't."

She leans in to kiss him with her rancid breath.

"What do you want?"

He grabs her thighs and turns her around onto her knees.

"I'm worried I'll shit a little on you."

"I don't mind," he says.

She helps him moisten her anus with spit and vaginal fluid. He pushes on through her sphincter, eliciting a burst of flatulence as it tightens around the base of his penis. He leans over her, thrusting in and out, grasping her crotch, rubbing her clit with his free hand. He feels her stomach shudder as she orgasms in silence. Her muscles contract around his penis. He pulls out of her and masturbates, ejaculating on the dry ground. He steps away and urinates. The girl lies face down still with her buttocks spread.

"Did I shit on you?"

"No," he says.

"It feels like I shit."

"It just felt that way," he says, adjusting his pants to sit down beside her.

"What was that we just did?"

"It's called sodomy."

"I'm not sure I liked it that much."

"Sorry," he says. "There might be a little blood next time you shit. That's normal. Your ass might burn for a while too. It'll go away."

"How do you know?" she says. "You ain't a doctor."

"I know from experience."

"You fuck all the girls this way?"

He sighs.

"No," he says. "I've not had an easy life."

"Who has?"

"A man did terrible things to me when I was too young," he says.

"I'm sorry. I know what that's like. My father used to hold me down," she says.

"You could have told me you didn't like it when I was doing it. I would have stopped."

"I still wasn't sure what I thought. Why don't you pour some whiskey on my ass to keep it clean?"

"You don't want to do that, trust me," he says, staring at her reddened, shut asshole.

She pulls herself up and sits uncomfortably on the ground to lean against him and stare at the flowering cactus.

"That's beautiful," she says.

"I've never seen anything like it."

The girl said her name was Florentina. He asked her if she was Mexican. She looked Mexican to him, not that he knew exactly what a Mexican looked like. Some people had a look and other people could look like anything and he never really understood why. The one-handed woman who more or less raised him didn't have much of an idea herself. She seemed to think that people with lighter skin and brighter colored hair were better than everyone else. She called it the virtue of western civilization, but she could not tell him what western civilization was or why it mattered. Another killer, a half-Zuni half-Shoshone woman he had worked with years ago, explained the history of the continent to him but it was difficult to keep it all straight so much had happened.

"Time is not a straight line. It curves and circles back. Sometimes it stops dead," she said. "My people were almost wiped out more than once."

"By who?"

"The American government."

"The Nazis?"

"Almost. But the Ethnostate came later. But the first Nazis were over in Europe and did the same thing there."

"Complicated."

"It's all pretty complicated."

Florentina, as it turned out, did not speak Spanish and she didn't know what she was or where her people, if she had any, came from.

He left in the early morning after sleeping alongside the girl. He stepped out of the camper before the sun came up after leaving some extra money on her side table.

The desert turns to chaparral the closer he rides to the outpost. He starts to see more trees and mountains in the distance. His camel is fed and properly hydrated and goes the entire day without water or food. He sleeps beside it, the cold night tucked away in a crevasse-like dip in the earth, hidden from the all-encompassing view.

The following day, he finds a fresh corpse amid the low vegetation. He draws his sidearm and swaps the magazine for a full one, sticking the partial into the leather loop on the gun belt. He chambers a round and keeps the barrel pointed at the sky with his index finger flat on the trigger guard.

Insects swarm over the sporadic bullet holes in the dead man's back.

He can't see anything above the ridge. Anyone could be waiting in the scrub. The camel appears calm for now and he signals for it to rest and fold in its massive legs so he can dismount. He crouches low and approaches the rotting corpse. The smell is unmistakable. The murder is fresh. The body is limp and supple and yet he heard no gunshots in the distance. He lifts the shoulder to check for exit wounds. Two of the six shots passed through. He unfolds his knife and digs into the meat of his back to see if he can pluck out a round. He holds the mashed bullet in his bloody hand and hazards a guess as to the caliber: perhaps a 9mm Parabellum. It was definitely a handgun, which puts him at ease. The ridge was a perfect hideout for someone with a rifle. He wipes his hands in the scrub and keeps going, steering the camel to the left to hopefully bypass whatever trouble that dead man had found.

9

He camps for the night under a honey mesquite and sets up a small fire to cook a can of beans and tin of spam. As he eats in silence, a Chinese soldier on horseback rides by the camp.

"Hey friend, nǐ huì shuō zhōngwén ma?" he says.

Pancho twirls the fork in his hand as he swallows.

"Not really. And I'm not your friend, friend," he says.

"Sounds like you understood what I said just fine," the Soldier says in an American accent.

"You pick up a little here and there."

The horse clops toward the crackling fire. The camel grunts. Pancho sets his food down and puts his hand on his gun.

"Don't come any closer."

The soldier raises his hands.

"I mean no harm. I got a pack of cigarettes in my pocket here. You want one?"

"I don't. I want you to leave me alone."

"I was hoping to trade."

He doesn't look like he has anything to trade. A lone soldier in the dead of night has "deserter" practically marked on his back. He probably got the horse off the dead man from earlier.

"I'm not making trades," he says, flicking the thumb safety on the pistol.

The soldier smiles.

"You're sure? A Lesser Panda cigarette is a fine smoke."

"I don't smoke tobacco cigarettes. They hurt my throat."

"Here, take a sniff," he says, reaching into his shirt.

As his hand disappears into his clothing, Pancho draws his pistol and fires four thunderous rounds. The soldier drops from his saddle before the last of the spent cartridges scatter along the rocks. The horse neighs and circles the fire. His camel grunts and bites at the air. Pancho stands and steps over to the dying soldier. He kicks his hand free from his shirt and sees the shoulder holster with the cheap, plastic Beretta copy.

He coughs and spits blood.

Pancho removes the pistol and takes the pack of cigarettes and the modest stack of cash off of his person before shooting him one last time.

The last shot perturbs the horse enough that it finally races off into the night. He whistles after it hoping to take it back to the outpost but it never returns.

He finishes his food and douses the fire.

10

The air is strangely cool once he reaches the military outpost. Frigid mist rolls off the mountainside in short swells carried by the southbound wind. A gathering of near-black rain clouds at the opposite peak crawl toward the sky over the modest, wooden building. Gray lightning erupts from within their dark girth. The Chinese flag thrashes on the aluminum poll, tearing in the violent wind.

The camel's fur dampens and flutters as they approach.

The outpost is still, lifeless. The lights are off. There's a single all-terrain vehicle in the gateway, but no camels or pack mules in the small enclosed stable. No Humvees. He sees no one in the watchtower either. The mounted rifle with the scope tilts upward like an unused telescope. Wasn't there supposed to be someone charged with telling him where the fracking site was hidden? He takes out his waterproof map and the photograph of the outpost and knows he's in the right place: Wan Shui, what the locals called Crying Rock.

"Carajo."

The rain sets in and he drapes his tarp over the saddle after stabling the camel. There's hardly any hay or water so he drags the empty rain barrel out in the open. He puts on his poncho and hides the Benelli underneath it, collapsing the retractable stock as he approaches the back entrance.

The center of the door has so many bullet holes it almost looks to have been eaten by termites. He pushes it open and the waft of carrion fumes keeps him back as he descends into the fit of coughing. The bodies, all soldiers except for one elderly American civilian, are strewn across the room past the point of rigor mortis, having rotted in the putrid heat before the cooler air arrived. He kicks aside spent shell casings and empty, slide-lock frozen pistols discarded in the middle of the merciless ambush.

Fuck 'em, he thinks. The job's bust. They'll need to send in a squadron if they want this mess handled properly.

He looks through a bullet hole in the window. The glass was cracked but not shattered, warped in a circular pattern like a spider's web. The rain seeps in through the weakened cracks. He steps over to another body. The dead soldier holds an MP-5 submachine gun with a banana magazine. Whoever killed him took the time to aim for the perfect shot: a single bullet between his eyes. The blowback from the exit wound paints the wall behind him. The viscous tissue, now suspended from its slow drip down the raw wood panel, looks almost like dried clay.

He is used to the difficulty of survival, the panic of an ambush. The furthest extremes of violence don't shake him, but the stillness here, the eerie quiet of this lingering aftermath, bothers him.

The small barracks are empty. He kicks open footlockers and canvas bags, not looking for any one thing in particular. He finds nothing. The darkened commissary briefly illuminates in the flash of the lighting. The thunder rattles the outpost. He searches for something to eat and finds a few tins of pinto beans and soft bamboo, squid saturated in oil and fermented duck eggs. He gathers up the food in a pillowcase and leaves through the side entrance. The thunder crashes overhead. He walks through the rain, thoroughly enjoying the cold, back toward the stable.

The camel grunts at him and he strokes its neck. When the rain barrel is full, he drags it back to the edge of the stall and removes the top. He sits in the open padlock doorway of the stable with his shotgun across his lap and watches the storm.

11

The bullet-riddled door creaks on its rusted hinges in the wind. The lightning and thunder lets up but the rain continues into the night. Pancho starts a small fire in the stable entranceway just beneath the watery spew of the eave and heats up the bamboo and beans inside his stew pot. When the mixture becomes thick, he opens the squid and oil and pours it into the simmering pot. Lastly, he peels a pine-colored duck egg and drops in the crumbled pieces for flavor. He stirs the hazmat stew together and sets the lid on top to keep it.

Behind him, the camel sleeps. Air passes through its sagging cleft lips.

He sees movement near the gateway and grabs his shotgun propped against the beam. He thinks he sees a creature, a coyote, or some kind of lizard crawling through rocks near the ATV.

A wounded soldier drags himself through the rain and rolls himself toward the sky with his mouth open, trying to drink.

Pancho treks out amid the crags to stand over him with the shotgun.

The soldier has multiple wounds: a bullet to the left shoulder wrapped in bloody gauze, soaked by the rain, and a useless broken leg, split by multiple gunshots, with a belt as a tourniquet at his kneecap.

"Nǐ..." is all he manages to say before Pancho interjects.

"Choi sent me. I came from Liang Yang."

"Gǔnkāi … "

"A little late for that. You even speak English?"

"I speak it just fine, fuck face. You're the one who's late."

Pancho lifts him up and helps the soldier hobble to the stable on his good leg.

"I thought everyone was dead," he says.

"Everyone is dead."

They make it to the stable and Pancho lays the soaked man beside the fire.

Pancho takes a seat on a wooden crate and stares at him with the shotgun across his lap.

"Anyone else still alive?"

"No."

"Choi sent me to neutralize someone who's making trouble around your illegal fracking site. Who is it? The Nation? Colorado Militia?"

The soldier laughs.

"Who? I don't know who's behind them. I can tell you who pulled the trigger."

"Who pulled the trigger?"

"You don't stand a chance."

"How many are there?"

"How many? How many?"

Pancho jerks the shotgun forward and shoots a slug into the earth by the soldier's head. A cloud of smoke and loose mud briefly covers his face.

"I won't ask you again and I certainly don't intend to miss a second time. One more body to add to that pile in there. Who's gonna miss you?"

"Alright, alright. Let me tell you. It's a long story."

"Find a way to make it short."

"It's just two people. That's it. That's all it is. I don't know who hired them, but it's just two people."

"You expect me to believe two people did this?"

"You'll find out soon enough if you stay here. And there's only one of them now."

"One?"

"We killed one."

"Is that why they came back and massacred this place?"

"Yes."

Pancho reaches for his plate and wooden ladle.

"So, who am I looking for?"

"A woman."

"A woman?"

He lifts the lid to the pot and stirs the simmering food.

"Black hair. Dark like you. Old."

"You're saying to me that the mysterious threat I've been hired to kill is an old lady?"

"It's the truth. Believe what you want."

Pancho smiles and places a ladle full of food on his plate.

"Were you playing dead back inside or were you hiding?"

"I was hiding."

"Hmm. Thought you were in the clear when you came out?"

"I heard the rain and I was thirsty."

Pancho stands up and enters the camel's stall. He flips over the tarp on the saddle. He takes out a canteen and another plate and utensils.

"You're gonna kill me anyway, aren't you?"

Pancho hands him the canteen. The soldier drinks frantically and wipes his mouth on his soaked sleeve.

"You want some of this?"

"What is it?"

"It's food."

He ladles a heavy plate for the soldier.

"I'm gonna get blood poisoning out here."

"You don't have a First-Aid kit in the barracks? Antibiotics? Medicine?"

"I've taken everything we have. It's the only reason I'm able to talk to you."

"Morphine?"

"Fentanyl cheek swab."

"That'll do it. I saw a man take one of those before they sawed his leg off."

"They'll have to do that to me if I don't die out here."

Pancho smiles.

"Eat up. Drink up. You'll need your strength for tomorrow."

"For what?" he says, poking at his food with a fork.

"I'll find a use for you."

The soldier hesitates before he eats.

Pancho eats in silence, happily chewing.

After a few bites, the soldier looks up at him and points to his food with the fork.

"Did you put a century egg into these beans?"

"I did."

"And calamari?"

"I just kind of dumped everything together to see how it'd turn out. Is it any good?"

"It's hot and it smells okay."

"I wasn't planning on sharing, so you get what you get."

The soldier eats reluctantly.

"Where are you from?" he asks.

"The desert," Pancho says. "How about you."

"Gansu. Right on the Yellow River."

"How long you been out here?"

"Fifteen years."

"Must have come over pretty young."

"I did."

"I came over pretty young too. Up from Mexico."

"You're Mexican?"

"I suppose so."

Pancho finishes his plate and washes it off in the falling rain. The soldier keeps eating as Pancho takes two industrial clamps to seal the pot. He throws two more sticks of wood on the fire and lights a stick of hemp for an after-dinner smoke. The herb crackles between his fingers as he inhales.

"Can you shoot?"

"I can shoot."

"If I put you behind a rock with a gun, you think you could cover me?"

"There's a lot of corners out here. Depends where you go. Even if you hit her, you might not kill her."

"Why not?"

"She wears Kevlar pads and a vest. Last time she had on a ballistics mask."

"I'll think of something."

12

Pancho keeps the dead body erect with duct tape and broken chair legs. Having removed his valuables from the saddle, he sends the camel out along the side of the valley with the body dressed in his rain poncho and hat.

He finds a spot behind a pair of rocks overlooking the valley where he plants the soldier with a rifle from the armory locker.

"You're sure this'll work?"

"She's liable not to trust a new face. It might stir something and bring her out," Pancho says.

He leaves the soldier in his perch, crawling down from the rocks.

The camel circles the grassy slope with the bait on its back.

He watches from a low hillock with the shotgun ready.

The sky is lighter but no sunlight shines through the clouds. A mild rain stops and starts as the hour passes.

The camel eventually saunters toward a soft patch of grass and collapses its leathery knees. The dead body wags back and forth and the hat droops over its face.

He whistles for the camel. Slowly, it pulls itself up and heads toward him.

A gunshot resonates through the valley. The camel bleats and foams at the mouth.

The body is intact. His camel appears unscathed. He cuts the body free from the saddle and lets it drop down like a pile of firewood.

Pancho smacks the camel's ass, letting it run back to the stable. He leaves his clothes on the corpse and creeps up the rocky crags to the soldier's hiding spot.

Blood stains the rocks. The soldier lies, face down, with a hole in his skull. The stalk of his Norico rifle is still pressed against his shoulder.

He keeps his back pressed against a tall rock with the shotgun ready. He wasn't patient enough, he thinks.

He stays behind the rock and waits and thinks.

A rainstorm comes and goes.

He waits.

13

A rock the size of a fist flies over his head. He thinks he sees a grenade at first and nearly jumps. She's trying to elicit a reaction, coax him into the open. He stays put.

A hawk screeches.

He gets down on his haunches and sighs audibly.

A rifle shot ricochets off the rock above his head. Another rebounds off the side.

He tries to follow the smoke trail but sees nothing left in the air. Leaning onto the side of the adjacent boulder, he fires off a volley of buckshot and then a rifled slug. The slug bounces off a jagged formation and hits the dirt by the soldier's feet.

"Looks like you and me are at an impasse," the female voice yells.

"Seems that way," he says.

"You wanna draw?"

"No," he yells. "I'm not stupid. You got on a vest and a mask."

"You see me?"

"No, the last man standing from the outpost told me. The man you just killed."

She hesitates.

"And you want revenge now?"

"It's not personal," he says.

"Who hired you?" she says.

"Who do you think? Who hired *you*?"

"Shoshone branch of The Nation."

He sighs.

"Really? No lies?"

"Why would I lie about that?"

He hesitates before he speaks.

"Well, looks to me like you've already won. If I leave here today, you promise not to shoot me in the back?"

He gets no answer.

"How about it? I know when I'm outmatched."

Silence.

He loads two buck-shot shells from his pocket.

He mumbles to himself.

"I'd have taken that deal."

He hears a lone, solid footstep on the rocks beside him and turns. The long barrel of a Winchester meets his chin.

She stands over him wearing thin, travel-worn clothes beneath her bulletproof vest. Her long black hair falls across her shoulders and her dark eyes stare at him through the featureless black mask, down the sights on the lever-action rifle.

"Drop the shotgun," she says.

He pulls the trigger.

The slug tears into the Kevlar vest, knocking her off the boulder. She falls flat on her back.

Pancho leaps onto the same spot, firing both slug and buckshot rounds. She rolls away and rises on her knees, returning fire with the Winchester. A 30-30 round penetrates his forearm. He drops the shotgun and slides down the boulder, fighting to pull the pistol from his holster. He draws it and hits the ballistic mask between her eyes. White material shows through the black outer layer.

She rips off the mask. He can see a bloody welt from the impact of the bullet. Blood trickles down her nose.

He studies her face through the sight of his pistol and then lowers his aim.

She looks at him and wipes the blood from her face.

"Jesus Christ," she says. "Pancho?"

He catches his breath.

"That's me."

"Do you remember me?"

"I remember you," he says "I don't remember your name."

"Amalin," she says. "You learned English."

He spits.

"You broke my arm," he says

"You probably broke my rib and gave me a concussion."

"Shit," he says, staring up at the gray sky.

14

Her face is ravaged by the years. A long knife scar cuts through the wrinkles below her left eye like a dried-up canal. Pancho studies her and tries to remember what she looked like when he was a child. She doesn't bother to do the same. She can already see the boy she took away years ago.

"You were always a natural shot," she says.

"My shooting days are clearly over," he says, gesturing toward the sling holding his shattered, duct-taped forearm. The circulation in his arm is all but cut off by the cloth tourniquet tightened by a wooden stick. "Good thing, you only shot the left one. I can still eat and wipe my ass."

"You can't shoot with your right?"

"I can," he says. "At least with a pistol."

She stirs the pot of food on the fire and then reaches into her pack.

"I can get you to The Nation and see if we can fix it."

Pancho finishes his smoke and tosses the butt into fire.

"This can't be fixed. It needs to be sawed off before it gets infected. At least I'll still have my elbow. Time to invest into a hook of some sort."

She takes out a bottle of whiskey.

"Drink?"

"Please," he says, reaching for the bottle. He takes a long drink at full tilt and hands it back. He points to the tarnished silver pistol in the leather holster across her waist.

"Hell of a gun right there."

"You know where I got it."

"The man who took me from my parents?"

She shakes her head.

"No," she says. "This gun. This belt. All of it. I took it off The Teacher after I snapped his neck. Took me two tries to kill him."

"So it was you. This whole time, it was you who destroyed Alberta City," he says, smiling.

"I didn't destroy anything. I just killed a stupid man."

"What about the other guy. The man with the truck?"

She grimaced.

"I got him out of Alberta. We drove out into the desert without supplies. The Nation, back then, wouldn't help us. I don't blame them. The Nazis got him. I got away. I was lucky."

"So you left me there?"

"You said you were from there."

"Yeah, but I didn't want to go back. I wanted to stay with you."

"I had a man to kill, Pancho. If you had stayed with me it would have been the same as staying with the man I took you from."

"Someone paid you to kill The Teacher?"

She scoffs.

"Never saw a dime. But I got my revenge."

"I remember more than I thought I did," he says. "Hand me that bottle again."

She tosses the bottle over the fire and he takes another drink. Amalin stokes the fire.

"What happened after we left you there in the walled city? How'd you grow up."

"Some white folks took me in and clothed and fed me. Started teaching me English and how to read and all."

"Treated you like their own?"

"No, not by a longshot. No, I ate what was left over and wore what they had torn. I slept outside most nights on a palate with a .22 by the side for snakes and coyotes. This old bag with one hand smacked my knuckles with an iron rod if I made a mistake reading."

"And the town?"

"The walls stayed up for a few more years and then resources dried up and we took off for another settlement near the refugee camps run by the UN. A group of camel breeders were offering money to kill a militia man for an alleged rape. After that, I heard about the bounty money the Chinese were putting on people and I didn't look back. I murdered someone in a gang after a fight in a camp and had an unofficial bounty on my head for a few months when I got to Bear Ears. The local Nation offered to help me kill off the gang members if I agreed to help them. We killed every last one of them."

Amalin ladles the broth-heavy soup into two bowls with tosses Pancho a wooden spoon.

"Sounds like you and I went into the same profession."

Pancho says nothing and screws the cap back on the bottle.

The sun falls behind the mountain in the distance and the fire becomes their only light. They eat and finish the pot of soup between them. Pancho offers her a Lesser Panda cigarette.

"I don't smoke," she says.

"I don't smoke these, but I'm out of my green leaf," he says and lights a cigarette with a match.

Amalin reaches for the whiskey and pours some into a chipped enamel cup.

"You ever wonder how the world got like this?" she says.

"Like what? Things are what they are."

"No," she says. "Not when I was young. Things were different. People had more. People had lives."

"People have lives now."

"It's hard to explain to people your age."

"Maybe people your age just remember it wrong."

"No, not like this. I used to work in a bookstore. I shared a house. I had my own shower. Girlfriends. Music. A computer."

"I've heard it all before," Pancho says. "I was a rich man and now I'm poor. Those days are long gone and we aren't getting 'em back."

He spits and takes a drag of the cigarette.

"It could have been avoided. It could have been helped."

"Yeah, but it wasn't," he says, rolling over on his back.

She sips her whiskey.

Pancho finishes the cigarette, sucking the last puffs of smoke from the filter, and then tosses it into the fire.

"That was good soup. What was that?"

"Water. Chicken bouillon powder. A little camel fat and wild mushrooms."

"That was a good meal," he says.

"What will the Chinese do to you if they find out you didn't kill me?"

"They won't find out. I'm sure they'll think I'm dead. And I have no problem with letting them think so."

15

In the morning, he wakes her up with his crying.

"What's wrong?"

"What do you think?" he says with tears in his eyes. "It's my arm. It hurts worse than when you shot it."

She stares at the swollen forearm and his limp, blood-caked wrist.

"You want another drink?"

"You need to go to those outpost barracks and find me dope and a hacksaw. It's got to come off."

"We need to wait until I can get a doctor to look at it."

"How many miles away is that? I can't ride like this."

"Sawing it off won't make it feel any better."

"I can't bear this pain!"

She helps him up and he screams even harder at the slightest movement of his forearm.

"Yeah, that's a 30-30 round. Pretty much mashed the bone to pieces. There's a sharp piece of bone slicing up your torn ligaments. You're still bleeding too."

"Ahh! You bitch, shut your mouth."

He collapses onto his knees.

*   *   *

She finds no dope in the barracks. The wounded soldier had used up everything for his leg. Instead, she force-feeds Pancho half a bottle of whiskey and ties him to his camel with bungee cord. She mounts her own Bactrian camel and leads them through the Rockies.

The animals foam at the mouth as they trek into higher elevation. The two-humped camel is used to climbing, but Pancho's hybrid lags behind in stubborn protest. Halfway up a sharp ridge, the camel refuses to go any further, whining and spitting like a wounded dog. Amalin connects the reins to her saddle in an attempt to lead it. The camel bites at her shoulder.

Pancho is passed out, slopped to one side putting tension on the cords. She adjusts his body and caresses the camel's neck. It doesn't reciprocate the affection.

After a delay, the camel follows her but never once stops screaming.

Pancho eventually wakes up in agony and starts drunkenly crying with the camel.

16

She takes out her binoculars and scans the circle of trailers across the plateau. Electric light shines through the plastic blinds behind the reinforced windows. There's a wooden post with a motion sensor floodlight a few yards to the right of the circle, registering the motions of nocturnal cats scampering after rodents. It's like looking back in time; a standard RV park. She sets up a rudimentary camp and lets the camels rest in the darkness. She fires a shot from her pistol in the air.

A shimmering orange flare rises in the dead night sky near the rectangular structures.

She fires two more shots in response.

An engine revs in the distance and moves toward her. Amalin peels the lid off a can of smoked mussels and eats them with a plastic fork.

"Are we under attack?" Pancho says.

"No."

"Kill me," he says.

"Shut up."

An old Subaru pickup truck rolls along the grass, switching to their low beams, lighting the camels who stir and grunt in its presence. The engine idles. Two men with Masada rifles strapped across their chests exit the back of the truck. The driver stays put.

"Amalin?"

She nods and finishes her food.

"Is this Frank?"

"Frank's dead," she says. "This is Pancho. He's my son."

"Your son?"

"Yeah, he's hurt. You wanna un-strap him and take him to Dr. Walsh?"

The two men look at each other.

"The contract was for you and Frank?"

"And the contract was fulfilled. Frank didn't make it. Give his share to his family and give me mine. My son isn't part of it. This is a favor I'm asking."

The two of them deliberate in Neo Numic.

The older man looks back at her, tapping his finger against the trigger guard of his rifle.

"Okay, bring him in."

She pulls out her knife.

"I'll cut him down and you rush him to medical. Then I'll stable the camels."

"You're not stabling shit. You come with us and your son. Derek will put up the camels."

"Even better," she says, sawing at the bungee cord.

They lift Pancho from the saddle and lay his body in the truck bed. The younger man stays behind as they drive full speed across the grass toward the camp.

186

Pancho stares up at the night sky and feels the truck chassis bounce. He's sick, dehydrated, and delirious. His arm no longer hurts and he isn't sure what that means.

17

Dr. Quincy Walsh isn't indigenous. He's an old black man with a long white beard and a shaved head. His nurse is Shoshone. He doses Pancho with the first of several injections. Pancho asks him how long he's had refuge within the Nation.

"Since the beginning," he says in a raspy, diminished cadence. "I'm former IHS."

"That some kind of elite death squad?"

The old doctor smiles.

"No, it stands of Indian Health Services."

Pancho looks confused.

"Young man like you, probably never heard the term Indian before."

"I know where India is."

"That's what I thought," he says, placing the mask over Pancho's face. "Take in a deep breath."

Pancho drifts and loses time. He sees things as his senses consolidate into varied synesthesia.

18

He wakes up in a cot covered with white sheets in the center of an airplane hangar. He can see the hills and a distant mountain through the opening. An IV drip dangles over him. Echoing footsteps approach him and the Shoshone nurse replaces his catheter. He doesn't have the strength to speak. He watches her as she hooks the new bag for urine and takes away the full pouch. The IV tube is stuck in the crook of his elbow below the wounded arm. He can't see it beneath the sheets and he can't feel much of anything. The sunlight pours in from the open threshold. He closes his eyes.

19

He wakes up and sees the doctor sitting on a small wooden stool beside his IV stand. The unobstructed stars shimmer over the hills through the half oval entrance of the hangar. Static electricity builds like razor-edged dust hidden within the seams of the sheets and clothing. The fabric clings to his legs and raises his hairs. The doctor is alone and drinking from an aluminum water bottle.

"How long has it been?" Pancho says through dry lips.

"Two days."

He leans his back on the pillow.

"Am I going to die?"

The doctor scoffs.

"No, you'll be fine. In fact, you're a walking miracle."

"How?"

"The bullet, as big as it was compared to your arm, didn't nick any arteries and the bone was hardly fractured."

"She said the bone was shattered."

"Who? You mother? Based on what?"

"It felt shattered."

"I'm sure it hurt like a son of a bitch, but it was pretty easy compared to the bullet wounds I've seen before. People die out here after getting shot in the foot. The bullet exited through your arm too. Came out clean. Can't ask for much better."

"What's with all this shit then?"

"You were severely dehydrated. And you lost a good amount of blood."

Pancho lifts his head.

"I feel strange."

"Painkillers. They'll do that. You don't seem to have much of a tolerance to them. Antibiotics too."

"Where's my guns and camel?"

"They're safe. You just need rest."

"So I get to keep my arm?"

"For now."

The doctor stands up slowly, resting his hands on his haunches as his body straightens. He kicks the stool to the side.

"That's a beautiful night sky out there tonight."

20

Once he's off the intravenous fluid and out of the gauze, the nurse comes and lays out his clean clothes and gun belt. They must have lost his hat because she hands him a new one, a bright tan Stetson. She fits his arm with a plastic splint to his forearm.

"It's going to hurt every night before you sleep and feel slightly better in the morning. You'll feel rain and storms coming before you can see the clouds."

"Like an old man," he says.

"Don't lift anything for a couple of weeks. And here," she hands him a plastic pouch with six pills. "Take two a day until it's finished and don't drink whiskey with them."

"For pain?"

"Medicine," she says. "If you don't take them, you could get sick and die."

"Alright," he says, taking the pills.

"You Shoshone or Comanche?"

He shakes his head.

"Mexican," he says.

"You know the Shoshone language is related to the Aztec language. Thousands of years ago, we might have been one people."

"What's Aztec?"

"It's Mexican. That's what Mexicans are, a mix of the Aztecs and other native groups with the European colonists and what not."

"Doesn't make me part of the Nation."

"You're here aren't you. You're alive."

"Good point," he says, wrapping his belt around his waist.

"What's Mexico like?"

"I couldn't tell you. I was only born there."

"You don't speak Spanish?"

"I can still speak Spanish."

The nurse strips the cot of the bed sheets.

Pancho slips into his boots and laces them.

"You don't get a lot of strangers here, do you?"

"What do you think?" she says, balling up the sheets. "You sticking around for a while? I'm sure we could find some work for you to do without using your left hand."

"No," he says.

"Your mother seems to think you are."

"She's not my mother, not my real mother at least. You do me one last favor?"

"Depends on what it is."

"Just bring me a pencil and a sturdy piece of paper."

She leaves the hangar and Pancho sits on the bare cot. It takes her a few minutes to return. She hands him a pen and sheet of parchment torn from a notebook. He pulls the stool between his legs and hunches over it with the pen like a small desk. Slowly, he writes.

When he's done, he folds the paper and hands the paper to
the nurse.

"Give that to Amalin," he says. "And tell me where my camel
and saddle are."

The nurse unfolds the paper and reads it.

"Does it make sense?"

She keeps reading.

"Been awhile since I wrote anything."

For Amaleen
Im sorry I haf tu go
they cant no Im here
the army will find owt Im
not ded You saved me
2 times now
Pancho

She finishes it.

"You have the Chinese army after you?"

"I will soon enough."

She tells him how to get to the stables and he staggers out
of the hangar.

21

He saddles the camel and fills his canteens and then rides out toward the sun along the grassy plain with his good hand on the horn of the saddle. He lets the camel move at its own pace. The clouds in the distance look like gods fighting in the sky. The girthy, whitish-gray plumes trade powerful blows of eternally suspended energy high above the mountains with their backs against the horizon. He ventures out along the tall grass and follows the babbling river. He checks his compass and follows the river further north. The water appears green. He sees the metallic remnants of the railroad and doesn't know what it is or what it was used for.

Amalin rides up beside him on a borrowed horse.

"I got your note."

"Yeah?"

"Why don't you stay. You've worked for the Nation before."

"Once you work with the Chinese though," he says. "Besides, I can't pay 'em for healing me."

"You don't have to leave. No one's asking you to."

"I know. But I'm still leaving."

"The Chinese army won't find out about it. That outpost isn't even supposed to exist."

"Not at first, but they'll find out about me soon enough."

"Where are you gonna go?"

"Wherever," he says.

"You're just gonna move along like a vagabond."

"I don't know what that means," he says.

He takes out the pouch and swallows his first antibiotic pill and chases it down with a swig from the canteen.

"You could help me kill more of them. They'll eventually send more here to work the site."

"I think you and the nation got it covered."

She turns the horse around.

"Alright then," she says. "Adiós."

"Adiós."

22

He leans on a pine trunk and looks out at the long sierra in the blue haze of dusk. The temperature drops from sweltering to frigid. He takes his time aligning stones to enclose a small fire with his right hand. He gathers twigs and sticks and two thick, dead branches which he snaps into quarters with his foot against a rock before stripping the paper from a few of his Chinese cigarettes, discarding the tobacco on the ground. The paper absorbs the match flame and ignites the kindling. He positions the branches over the meek flames in a cone shape and lets them collapse into the red coals as they wither and burst with floating orange embers. Famished, he blackens an expired can of succotash on the fire and scoops out the sweet corn, beans, and okra with his fork as steam rises from the opening. He takes another pill and drinks from his canteen. The antibiotics and succotash sour his stomach. He rests beside his sleeping camel and listens to his gut churn through the night. In his dreams, he sees himself as a child with a slingshot.

He wakes up at dawn with his stomach settled. He shits off in the brush and wipes himself with paulownia leaves. The camel grunts and refuses to stand. He lets it keep sleeping for another hour as he watches the sunrise. He counts his shotgun shells: five buckshot rounds and twelve slugs remain. He fills his magazine from the box of .45 ACP and adjusts his belt. He counts his money and he checks his rations.

He urinates to kill off that last smoldering coals of the fire and mounts the saddle. The camel rises to its feet and carries him out of the forest toward the bald hills of dried clay and stone out toward the Sierra. The sun beats down on him. He wipes his brow free of sweat and whistles to himself.

In the mid-afternoon, he encounters a freshly blazed trail parallel to a trickling creek. Birds of prey scream overhead and wild goats mew at one another from the high ground. He's unfamiliar with this kind of peace and, after enjoying his solitude for some time an inexplicable notion of danger takes over. The thin trunk of a tall water birch near the creek sways in the wind and he draws his pistol in anger. His camel is unstirred. He holsters the gun.

The trail leads to a small shantytown built atop the remains of an asphalt parking lot. Long weeds and stray brush rise up through the cracks in the sun-bleached pavement. He steers the camel through what at least appears to be the settlement's main road. People drenched in sweat gaze up at him on the camel saddle as they cross the half-finished boardwalks and cracked pavement. The town is made up of an amalgam of loose tents, concrete bunkers, and wooden shacks with old clapboard sides and tin roofing. A single adobe hut stands at the end of the short thoroughfare. There are two other camels with their reins tied to a warped bicycle rack. He ties up his own and peers in through the rubber-flap door to the inside. No one makes eye contact with him.

Aside from the elderly bartender sitting behind the folding table with his back to the bottles, Pancho is the only dark-skinned face. Everyone here is miraculously pale or burned pink by the sun. He approaches the folding table and reads the handwritten sign with the drinks and food available and their corresponding prices. He remembers the nurse telling him not to drink whiskey with his pills.

He pays the old man for a lemonade. The bartender pours him a glass of filtered water and uses a metal device to squeeze half a lemon before dropping half an alkaline tablet into the glass. The drink fizzes and foams with lemon pulp.

Pancho takes a massive gulp of the sparkling drink.

"*¿Hay un establo por aquí?*"

A white man in the corner with a glass of whiskey answers for him.

"There's no stable here for you, Mexican. There's no room for you either. Drink your drink and get the fuck out."

The rest of the clientele ignore him; either too docile to deal with him or too preoccupied to care. The bartender doesn't speak. Pancho wonders if the man is mute. He turns and eyes the young man who insulted him as he drinks his lemon soda.

"What are you staring at me for? No speakee American?"

"No, I understand. I just don't know why you're acting so strange. You drunk?"

The man wipes his wispy mustache and scoffs.

"How come you ain't drinkin'?"

"I'm taking medicine."

"Medicine? For what? Gonorrhea?"

"Gunshot."

He laughs.

"This asshole thinks he's a fuckin' desperado," he says and stands up only to stagger, nearly slipping as his knee buckles.

An older man gets fed up and helps him to his feet. He props him up by wrapping his arm around his shoulder and leads him out the door.

"You're done. You're done for the day," he says.

Pancho finds a seat and sips his drink and looks around the room, thinking to himself. No one apologizes to him and the bartender never answers his question about a stable. He finishes the drink and cleans out the bottom of the glass with his finger to eat the remnants of the alkaline tablet and a stray lemon seed. The patrons watch him in silent disapproval. He returns the glass and pushes through the rubber-flap door.

The same, drunk man is still hanging around outside, leaning against his camel as he takes a piss between the wedges of its toes. Instead of nipping at the man, the camel laps up the orange stream. He laughs as he zips his pants and turns to Pancho.

"Fuck you, wet back."

Pancho draws and shoots the man in the crotch. He falls back, blood pouring from between his legs. He writhes and screams, scrambling across the cracked asphalt. Two others exit the bar with pistols in their hands.

Pancho kills both, shooting them each in the head. Blood mists in the air and condenses on the adobe. He takes off on his camel. The hybrid races out of town, foaming at the mouth. The wounded man screams and fires off five rounds from his pistol in Pancho's wake.

23

He crosses an iron bridge over a river of polluted, copper-colored water. The stench of the chemicals and sewage rises in the sweltering heat. He coughs and wraps a bandana around his face. The smell barely subsides as he reaches the opposite bank. He follows the paved road into the center of an abandoned town. Vines wrap around street lamps and trees push up slabs of concrete in the hollow centers of brick buildings. Puddles of emulsified plastic stain the ground. He figures it's the furthest north he's ever traveled. The sun beats down on him as it did in the desert. He strokes his camel's neck after he finds a patch of grass to stop. It folds its knees and he dismounts. He ties up the reins on a crepe myrtle stump. The camel languishes, nibbling at the grass. Pancho walks through the town, kicking over warped scraps of metal and scattered branches from past storms. The shop fronts are all covered in the plywood boards where no glass remains. Confused, he pushes a few boards out of the way to see the empty frame where the windows had once been. The shelves are empty. Lizards and snakes disperse in his presence.

He keeps wandering until he finds a place to sit and drink his water in the town square beneath a willow tree. He imagines seeing cars and people surrounding him, he laughs to himself about shooting the man in the crotch. His humor is cruel and tasteless but appropriate for his circumstances. He shoots a squirrel down from the branch for dinner and spends the afternoon cleaning the carcass. He waits for sunset before setting up a fire, using the bushy tail fur to ignite the kindling. He roasts the animal on a stick in the growing darkness and eats the blackened meat. He sleeps and then wakes up before dawn and drinks more water.

Pancho leaves the town behind and rides out through an endless expanse of arid brush.

EPILOGUE

Pancho rides for another year, compulsively moving from town to town, never settling, living as best he can without working or spending too much money. His arm heals but he's never able to completely close his grasp in his left hand. The Chinese never send a tracker after him. He passes a base in the winter months on the fields of what was once called Oklahoma and the personnel who sell him water and supplies don't recognize him for any other traveler. He figures Choi and the rest of the brass at Liang Yang assume he's dead, or just don't care. Months before, the brother of the man whose testicles he shot back at the shantytown caught up with him in a small pueblo settlement near a UN aid center and met the same fate.

Through the next year, Pancho asks a woman in a moving trailer to shave his hair bald and his beard clean off, and by the summer his beard returns and his hair fills out once again. He learns to speak a little Cherokee while passing through parts of The Nation and trades his shotgun for a tent. He rides like he's running from someone, even after he figures he isn't a wanted man. It's a form of searching, he thinks to himself, though he's without the ability to articulate his neurosis any further. He builds hundreds of fires and spends hundreds of nights alone with his unnamed camel. On a rock overlooking a river in the former state of Texas, the camel bleats awkwardly, drops to its side, and dies. He pushes it off the cliff. At night, he counts his money by firelight and knows he doesn't have enough for a new camel. He spends eight days stranded in the canyons before mustering the strength to drag his saddle along like a giant tortoise shell to the next settlement. A group of young women find him collapsed in the sand by the side of a concrete bunker and take him into their sprawling tent to get him hydrated. It's the first time in months he's spoken to another human being. He explains that his camel died and he was looking to trade what valuables he could for lodging while he finds some potential work. The girls put him up in a hammock in exchange for his bowls and his cooking pot and tell him he can stay until he finds a job to do.

He spends the next few days wandering the nameless settlement asking about work and finally meets the son of a Moroccan camel breeder driving a caravan of eighteen camels down to Mexico on the order of a rich town leader. The young man asks him about his situation and the gun belt around his waist and determines, since Pancho already has a saddle, that he might be a good addition to the team in case they needed more protection from marauders. The caravan crosses the Rio Grande, entering Mexico. The majority of the camel herders are drifters themselves and Pancho finds himself in good company. At night most of them share stories of their difficult and strange lives across the ravaged continent. Some of them are old enough to remember cars and gasoline and amenities like indoor plumbing and running water. Pancho tells a few redacted stories about his life but never admits to killing for the Chinese government. They share whiskey and hemp cigarettes and cook over a hard fire. Pancho proves himself as a camel wrangler and works hard to speed up the process of breaking camp in the mornings after making the coffee.

As they head deeper into Mexico, two herders at the back of the caravan lose a camel to a rattlesnake. The Moroccan camel breeder announces he'll have to reduce everyone's pay since the order was specifically for eighteen camels. Two indignant men try to incite a quiet mutiny which the others flat-out refuse. Pancho keeps his mouth shut.

One night, he observes the same two men fighting after one accused the other of stealing a pair of socks. He almost gets between the two inebriated men but the camel breeder holds him back and tells him to let them kill each other.

"They're both dead weights anyway," he says. "I'll give you their shares."

He watches in silence as one kills the other with a rock. The victor rises to his feet with the alleged sock thief's blood on his shirt. The camel breeder draws his Sig Sauer P226 and fires a hollow point through his skull.

The caravan leaves the dead men's belongings behind and reaches their destination with seventeen Arabian camels. The rich client isn't a mayor or sheriff of any kind.

Armed men with featureless bulletproof masks interrogate the caravan on the outskirts of the pueblo city. He sees Amalin in every guard. After an hour of harassment, they escort the caravan to the stables before bringing the herders into the warlord's compound to receive payment. Pancho refuses to check his gun at the electric fence and waits for the rest of them outside. He stares down a hefty body guard as he smokes.

They leave the compound and the Moroccan hands Pancho his money to keep the others from noticing how much more it is.

"It was good working with you," he says. "You coming back up north with us?"

"No," he says.

He rides out the very same night after purchasing a new camel.

The next day, he stops at a small house with a well out front and knocks on the door. An older woman with a gray streak in her black hair peers out from the window brandishing a .357 magnum.

"What do you want?"

"I want some water. I'll pay you."

"Unhook that belt and kick it to the side."

He does as he's told.

"Don't move," she says, stepping out into the sun. "You want water?"

"And any food if you can spare it."

"Let me see the money."

He shows her the stack of bills.

"Who are you running from?"

"I'm not running from anyone. I came here to deliver camels to Don Malinche. I got paid and now I'm moving on."

"I don't trust anyone who works for Malinche."

"I don't work for him. I just sold him some camels."

She sneers.

"Alright, but I'll fill your canteens. You stand there and keep your hands where I can see them."

He does as she asks.

When she's finished setting the wet canteens into his saddle, he asks her how much he owes her. She wants ten dollars for the water.

He gives it to her.

"You got any food?"

"Yeah," she says in a softer tone. "Come inside. Leave your guns out here."

They walk into the dark kitchen and she takes out a roll of dried meat and wraps it in aluminum foil.

"Forty dollars," she says.

He pays her and takes the meat.

As he leaves, he takes his gun belt and rests it over his shoulder. She watches him disappear into the beige hills.

He likes the way she looked even though she was older and admires her independence. Strangely, she doesn't remind him of Amalin. He thinks about her as he rides, fantasizing about returning to have sex with her, lying beside her in her bed knowing full well that if she sees him again, she'll probably shoot him.

Unsure of his exact location in Mexico, he rides east and ends up crossing the Rio Grande again, returning to the former territories of southern Texas. He unearths an old road sign and reads the names of the long-forgotten cities and distance markers.

The new camel is easier to ride and more agreeable. He rides it nonstop for days until he runs out of land and finds himself surrounded by salty, wax-colored mud and leafless trees. The wind blows too hard to keep his hat and he stashes it with his belongings. The camel trudges through the marsh, its feet submerged in estuarial water. He notices strange birds he's never seen before. He crosses a ridge of dunes and sees the brown and greenish water of the Atlantic for the first time. He watches the tide come and wash the mud from his camel's feet. He takes off his boots and rolls up his pants to feel the muck and salt water between his toes.

He returns to the grasslands in the coming months and buys a new automatic shotgun. Having spent all of his money, he winds up searching for more work in a hippie ashram. The descendants of environmental activists task him with protecting their vegetable gardens, corn, and cannabis fields. They pay him in food and shelter, housing him in a wooden shack on the edge of the corn field. They talk differently than him and don't allow him to carry guns within the communal areas. Over time, he builds his own rudimentary stable beside his shack with the help of a few young men. He lets their children ride his camel in the evenings when the ashram gathers to play forgotten music. The women try to loan him books to read and try to teach him about crystals and healing herbs. A few women find him intriguing and he asks if any of them might want to move into the shack with him, but no one does. He lives alone for a year, staying put despite his disconnection from the rest of the ashram.

In the dead of night, a little girl, half-naked, blood running down her legs, emerges from the corn stalks. Awakened by her screams, he shines a lantern out into the field and sees her. He takes her from the dirty ground and wraps her in a linen sheet, asking her what happened. She says nothing. He takes her to the ashram to find her mother. Two women tend to the scraps on her knees and the bottoms of her feet. Pancho sees what's been done to her and searches the different communal barracks and private rooms for anyone missing. One of them, a tall man with red hair, the girl's uncle, returns under the cover of darkness. Pancho intercepts him before he can get inside his room, dragging him out into the center of the commons beside the fire pit. Half the ashram gathers to mitigate Pancho's violence. He accuses him of raping the girl. Her uncle denies it. Pancho asks him where he was all night and he claims to have been fishing alone. He asks him why he's covered in dirt like the little girl.

"Because you forced me out here," he says.

Pancho challenges him to take off his pants so he could see if the girl's blood is still on him.

The man goes silent.

No one else challenges him, but no one offers to help either.

A friend of Pancho's, a man who helped build the stable, asks him not to kill him.

Pancho scans the faces in the crowd.

"I'm gonna kill this man," he says. "Try and stop me."

"If you murder him, we'll have no choice but to banish you."

The girl's uncle seizes his chance and runs away toward the fields. Pancho races after him, heading to his lonesome shack where he bursts through the door and retrieves his pistol. He catches up quickly, galloping through the corn and tall hemp stalks.

The man whimpers and pleads as he gains on him.

The two trample the stalks and enter a clearing. Pancho aims and shoots him in the leg, stopping him cold.

He screams for help.

Pancho catches his breath and looks over his shoulder. No one comes to aid either of them. He closes in with the gun snug in his hand.

The red-haired man stops professing his innocence. Instead, he asks for mercy. He begs for his life and admits to what he did. He grovels at Pancho's feet, crying, asking for forgiveness. He collapses underneath the barrel of the gun as Pancho hesitates and pulls his feet away from the cowering man.

"Please don't kill me!"

He pulls the trigger and walks away.

The second bullet splits his opposite kneecap.

The girl's uncle drags himself halfway to the ashram before bleeding out.

In the morning, a wake of vultures circle the field and swoop down to feed on the carrion.

Pancho loads his belongings on his saddle and sets out before breakfast. The commune elders catch him as he leaves. They offer him food and an extra blanket.

At the top of the hill, he looks back at the vegetable gardens and sees a woman who used to cook for him and tend to his insect bites. He waves goodbye and steers the camel toward the coming storm.

THE END.

ABOUT THE AUTHOR

Connor de Bruler lives in South Carolina.

www.ingramcontent.com/pod-product-compliance
Lightning Source LLC
Chambersburg PA
CBHW020321260626
47156CB00004B/1319